D0783666

HANS CHRISTIAN
ANDERSEN
Fairy Tales

Vol. 1

VOLUME 1

HANS CHRISTIAN
ANDERSEN
Fairy Tales

Published in Co-operation
with the Hans Christian Andersen
House, Odense.

Translated from the original Danish text by
R. P. KEIGWIN

Illustrations by
VILHELM PEDERSEN
and LORENZ FRØLICH
*reproduced from the original drawings in
the Andersen Museum at Odense*

SKANDINAVISK BOGFORLAG
FLENSTED
ODENSE . DENMARK

This edition of
Hans Christian Andersen's Fairy Tales
is being issued from Odense,
the poet's native town,
by the publishing firm of
Skandinavisk Bogforlag and Flensted

ISBN 87 7010 027 6 Export Edition complete
ISBN 87 7010 029 2 Library Edition volume I
ISBN 87 7010 028 4 Library Edition complete
ISBN 87 7010 033 0 Luxury Edition volume I
ISBN 87 7010 037 3 Luxury Edition complete

Printed in Denmark

CONTENTS

INTRODUCTION
by
ELIAS BREDSDORFF, M. A.
(Lecturer in Danish to Cambridge University)

It might seem superfluous to add yet another English translation of Hans Christian Andersen's stories and fairy-tales to the many already existing, when one considers that scores and scores of English and American translators have tried their hand at Andersen since the first English translations of his fairy-tales were published in 1846. A closer examination of these previous translations would, however, convince anyone with a knowledge of the original Danish text that this new translation by Mr. R. P. Keigwin is badly needed. The majority of the previous English translations tend to create such a misconception of Andersen's genius, that although they have given Andersen an unparalleled popularity and made his name 'a household word', they have at the same time done irreparable damage to his literary prestige in the English-speaking world.

It took England and America a hundred years to discover the Danish philosopher Søren Kierkegaard, whereas Kierkegaard's slightly older contemporary, Hans Christian Andersen, was 'discovered' in England and America at a remarkably early date. Andersen's novel, 'The Improvisatore'—for even in England he was first known as a novelist—appeared in English translation in 1845, when the author himself was no more than forty years old. From the contemporary reviews, as well as from other sources (e.g. the love-letters of the Brownings), we can see how much serious interest Andersen aroused in the literary world in England at this time. When Andersen paid his first visit to England and Scotland in the summer of 1847 the reception he received was quite overwhelming. In London he shared with his friend Jenny Lind, the Swedish singer, the fatiguing honour of being lionized to an extent which he had never experienced before. But most important of all, in London he met Charles Dickens, who had come up from the country with the sole purpose of meeting Andersen, whose stories Dickens loved and admired. "Whatever you do, don't leave off writing, for we cannot afford to lose any of your thoughts. They are too purely and simply beautiful to be kept in your own head," Dickens wrote in a letter to Andersen in 1847. Ten years later, Andersen came to stay as Charles Dickens's guest at Gad's Hill for five weeks. That proved a little too much for Dickens, for his Danish visitor had a very limited vocabulary in English, and was therefore rather tiresome to entertain for such a long period. But the friendship and mutual admiration of these two great writers is a lasting and important Anglo-Danish link; and the sincere admiration for Andersen's stories and fairy-tales, expressed by such different English and American authors as Charles Dickens, H. W. Longfellow, Elizabeth Barrett Browning, Walt Whitman, Oscar Wilde,

9

Hilaire Belloc, and G. K. Chesterton, is worth remembering at a time when there is an increasing tendency—both in Britain and in America—to disregard Andersen as a man of literary importance, and to label him exclusively as 'a nursery writer', a harmless entertainer for the little ones—with the tacit implication that Andersen has nothing to give to the adults.

For such is the situation in Britain to-day —and I believe also in America. Hans Christian Andersen's stories and fairy-tales have increasingly become the prey of unscrupulous publishers speculating in cheap and popular 'nursery books'. One such edition after another of 'Andersen's Fairy Tales', paying no regard to the author's artistic and moral intentions, is published in editions of hundreds of thousands. In many cases, therefore, it is a distorted and mutilated Andersen we meet in these books. Very often the editors and translators present to their readers a bowdlerized Andersen, with bits left out here and there, and other bits—freely invented and quite out of tune with the real story—

put in at random. The literary style of these translations is too often nothing but a scrap-heap of stale phrases and hackneyed clichés; for the translators, or adaptors, have dressed Andersen up in their own tiresome and uninspired literary garments. Among all the many doers-into-English of Andersen there are only a few who have known their job and made a genuine effort at an artistic re-creation of Andersen's exquisite prose in English. Some of the Victorian translators, who felt it their duty to polish, adapt, and even rewrite him, openly state that their version is 'told to the children', or 'set forth in simple words for little children', or 'retold in words of one syllable'; or we find that the tale has been 'arranged' or 'adapted' by some well-intentioned literary hairdresser. In such cases one is warned, at least, and knows what to expect. It is far worse when the transla-tions pretend to be genuine English render-ings of Andersen, when so often they are not. In a recent edition of *The Little Match Girl* Andersen's name is given without qualifica-tion as the author, although in fact the translator has given the story a happy ending, so that "the little match girl does not die from the bitter cold, but finds warmth and cheer and a lovely home where she lives happily ever afterwards"!

'The True Wizard of the North'—that was the term Mr. E. V. Lucas said he would rather apply to Hans Christian Andersen than to Walter Scott: "because whereas Scott took men and women as he found them, the other, with a touch of his wand, rendered inhuman things—furniture, toys, flowers, poultry—instinct with humanity." In most of the popular English and American editions of Andersen there is very little left of that wizard, and his magic wand has often been replaced by a raised admonitory finger.

Andersen's stories are infinitely more than their 'plots'. It is not enough for a translator of Andersen to have a good knowledge of Danish, although that, of course, is essential. (Many of the earlier translators did not even have that; some of them did not know any Danish at all, and made their translations from German versions, or, as some of them boldly wrote, "from the original German of Hans Christian Andersen"! Others were lacking in their knowledge of English.) Any good translator must be familiar with Andersen's writings generally, he must realise that Andersen was deliberately addressing himself in his stories as much to the grown-ups as to the children, and that the grown-ups will often understand much more than the children. He must achieve a full understanding of Andersen's style, which was nothing less than a revolution in his own time; he must fully understand his humour—perhaps the most essential key to his genius—and he must know the personal, biographical background of each story, for the stories abound in personal allusions, which may not matter to the uninitiated reader, but which should nevertheless be correct for anyone who wants to find them. Mr. R. P. Keigwin, who has devoted himself for many years to the study of Danish literature and has made a large number of excellent translations from Danish into English, fulfils all these requirements, and I cannot think of anyone better equipped to translate Hans Christian Andersen into English. His new version of the first four tales from Andersen, published in 1935 by the Cambridge University Press in commemoration of the centenary of their first appearance in Danish, was rightly praised by the critics both for the loyalty to the author's text and intentions, and for its own literary quality. His version, together with the translations by the late Paul Leyssac, and the recent American translation by Jean Hersholt, are among the very few exceptions to the rule that the English translations of Andersen fall far below the originals.

Hans Christian Andersen's stories and fairy-tales are world literature in the truest sense of the word. It is as wrong to limit their influence to the nursery as it would be to limit Dean Swift, Charles Dickens, and Lewis Carroll to the nursery. Andersen was the creator of a true poetry, so universal that many of its expressions are even to-day equally fascinating to an Odense child, an English child, and a Hindu child, and very little of it has become dated. Hilaire Belloc once wrote about Andersen: "I will bargain that if our letters survive five hundred years, this excellent writer will quietly survive." He defined Andersen's threefold genius as follows: "in the first place, he always said what he thought; in the second place, he was full of all sorts of ways of saying it; and, in the third place, he said only what he had to say." Andersen himself once defined the literary genre in which he was, and still is, the unsurpassed master, in these words: "In the whole realm of Poetry no domain is so boundless as that of the fairy-tale. It reaches from the blood-drenched graves of antiquity to the pious legends of a child's picture-book; it takes in the poetry of the people and the poetry of the artist. To me it represents all poetry, and he who masters it must be able to put into it tragedy, comedy, naive simplicity, irony, and humour; at his service are the lyrical note, the childlike narrative and the language of nature description ... In the folk-tale it is always Simple Simon who is victorious in the end ... Thus also the Innocence of Poetry, overlooked and jeered

15

at by the other brothers, will reach farthest in the end."

It was time that Andersen should be rediscovered in the countries where his phenomenal success—judging from the many editions and the number of printed copies—is so overwhelming that it has almost obliterated his true genius. For this reason I greet with great satisfaction the publication of this new translation of some of the best of Andersen's tales. In my opinion, this new version by Mr. Keigwin brings the fantasy and poetry of Hans Christian Andersen's universe as close as any translation can do it to all those who can read Andersen's tales only in English: that universe which is so different from the actual one in which we live our daily lives, and yet so teasingly like it— a poetic universe where Andersen—to quote that critic and essayist, Mr. Robert Lynd— "endows everything he sees—china shepherdesses, tin soldiers, mice and flowers— with the similitude of life, action and conversation. He can make the inhabitants of one's mantelpiece capable of epic adventures,

16

and has a greater sense of possibilities in a pair of tongs or a door-knocker than most of us have in men and women. He is a creator of a thousand fancies. He loves imagining elves no higher than a mouse's knee, and mice going on their travels leaning on sausage-skewers as pilgrims' staves, and little Thumbelina, whose cradle was 'a neat polished walnut-shell ... blue violet-leaves were her mattresses, with a roseleaf for a coverlet.' His fancy never becomes lyrical" [here I beg to differ] "or sweeps us off our feet, like Shakespeare's in *A Midsummer Night's Dream*. But there was nothing like it in the fairy-tale literature of the nineteenth century." And we can now add: nothing like in the first half of the twentieth century either.

Hans Christian Andersen has become part of our common European heritage; indeed, he has become world property, but he was eager that his readers should never forget that he was Danish. Therefore it is proper that this new version should be published in his native town of Odense. And I am sure that Andersen himself, with his deeply rooted love of his native Denmark, would have rejoiced had he known what Hilaire Belloc would write about him in 1910: "He was Northern; you always feel as you read him that if his scene is laid in the open air, the air is fresh and often frosty; that if he is talking indoors the room is cosy and often old. Certain passions which the North lacks are lacking in him, both upon their good and upon their evil side. He is never soldierly, and he is never revengeful; he is never acute with the desire for life, but, again, he is never envious. Those who read him and who are also Northern may well be in love with Denmark."

Cambridge, January, 1950.

HANS CHRISTIAN
ANDERSEN

On New Year's Day, 1835, Hans Christian
Andersen wrote to a woman friend: 'I
am now beginning some 'Fairy-tales for
Children', I shall try to win the future gene-
ration, you know!", and in a letter some-
time later, he mentions that of these stories,
they say "It is my Immortal Work".

These words from a young writer of 30
years of age, sounded prophetic, and time
justified them. Since the first edition was
published, the stories have been printed over
and over again: they are to be found
throughout the whole world, translated into
every important language.

The earliest of Hans Andersen's stories are
founded on folk-tales, but he did not simply
tell the same story—he developed and re-
created the folk-story, and thus he differs
from all other writers who have made use

in their writings of material from old fairy-tales.

About 1843, he changed over to his own original stories. "Now I tell stories with all my heart, get hold of an idea for the older folks, and then tell a story for the young folks, remembering all the time that father and mother often listen and we must give them something to think about, too! I have heaps of material, more than for any other kind of writing: it often seems to me as if every hoarding, every little flower is saying to me 'Look at me, just for a moment, and then my story will go right into you; and then, if I feel like it, I have the story.'

That is what happened. The inspiration of the fairy-tale could come from many places, from memories of childhood, from experiences on his travels, from small episodes occurring by the way. Such fairy-tale "seeds" are to be found scattered throughout his writings. They could lie buried in his mind for years. "They lay in my thoughts as a seed-corn, requiring only a flowing stream, a ray of sunshine, a drop from the cup of bitterness, for them to spring forth and burst into bloom."

Hans Andersen's fairy-tale writings also differ from folk-tales in the richness of their descriptions of nature. He had an exceptionally clear eye for the beauty of nature. Added to this, the stories ripple with humour. From first to last, one notices his wit in pointed and striking little remarks. The Soldier's friends in "The Tinder-Box", who deserted him when there were too many stairs to climb, the man in "Little Claus and Big Claus", who could not bear the sight of a parish clerk. The whole story can sometimes be a satire in itself as in "The Emperor's New Clothes" and "It's as True as True".

The fairy-tale was the form of art which could completely reveal Hans Andersen's special talent, and it was the tool which he could so ably use to reveal common human weaknesses and also—when occasion arose —to send his personal bugbears a little message. It has been said that every story contains something of the poet's life-blood, and for this very reason they are undying.

From this it will be understood, that there is a close connection between Hans Andersen's life story and his writings—the life story which he himself regarded as a fairytale, the story of the poor boy who became a celebrated poet of world-wide fame, the story of the ugly duckling that became a beautiful swan.

He was born in Odense, in Denmark, 2nd April 1805. His home was a poor one. His father was a shoemaker, imaginative and romantic. Traits in the father's character were inherited by his son. His mother was a big strong woman, who did the best she could to keep the little home together, and when Hans Andersen looked back on his childhood home through the coloured spectacles of memory it was enhanced in beauty. It was the circle of his childhood dreams. Here he played with the marionette theatre which his father had made for him. He made costumes for the puppets himself, and on the ideas from the theatre posters which were given to him, he wrote the plays. Only occasionally did he manage to go to the real theatre, where a new world of make-believe revealed itself to him.

Quite early he was known to be odd and different from other boys. He was "big and strange" like the ugly duckling and therefore he was an object of ridicule. He received only the scantiest of school learning, though in some subjects he was quite apt.

The Napoleonic Wars cast their shadow over his childhood home. His father succumbed to his urge for adventure and joined the army. Maybe financial circumstances compelled him to take this step. Hans Andersen's mother had to earn the daily bread by washing for people, and when his father returned home in a couple of years, he was so broken down in health that he died shortly afterwards. His mother married again, and the little Hans Andersen was left still more to himself.

He could sit by Odense River for hours at a time, dreaming of strange lands, as he watched the foaming water streaming over the wheels of the water-mill. Or he would sometimes accompany his grandmother to the hospital where poor elderly women sat spinning, and where he could listen to the tales they told, and also tell stories himself to impress them with his knowledge.

His childhood passed and he had to decide what he would be. His mother thought that he ought to learn a trade, and others advised him likewise. At that time, when there were very strong social distinctions, anything higher than this could not reasonably be contemplated for a boy who belonged to the lower strata of society.

But the boy's imagination carried him higher, and he made it clear to his family that he was going to be famous and that although he might have to go through terribly hard times, he was quite sure fame would come to him one day. The theatre was the object of his ambition. He remembered his marionette theatre, the plays he had been to at Odense Theatre, and people said that he had a nice voice. Down by the river, he had stood on a stone and sung in a loud voice to attract attention—in a garden nearby, there had been a party and several of the players from the Royal Theatre had been there. The Royal Theatre (he felt) must bring him the fame he strove for.

One day in September, 1819, the 14-year-old boy said good-bye to his mother and grandmother and set off for Copenhagen. He suffered hardships in the large unfamiliar city, but he managed to get taken as a pupil at the theatre to which he gave—then and always—an unhappy devotion.

But he was not to be an actor. His talent did not lie in this direction, and there came a day, after a couple of years at the theatre, when he was discharged from its service.

In the ordinary course of events one would think that Hans Andersen would now be quite helpless, and destined to sink to the bottom of society. He had no education or training that could help him to earn a living. He had not a single relation who could help him. But he had a burning faith in God who was sure to come to his aid, and he was determined to win through. It must have been this strange self-confidence that arrested the attention of influential people, and gained for him admission to circles which would otherwise have been closed to him.

That one of the directors of the Royal Theatre, Jonas Collin, interested himself in Andersen was of the greatest significance to his future career. He recognised that, first and foremost, it was necessary to give Hans Christian Andersen the knowledge and education which he lacked. He arranged for him to go to a Latin School. Steady work was not in Andersen's line, neither was it pleasant for him to sit side by side with much younger boys in a junior class. Again his schoolfellows found him 'big and strange'. After many trials and troubles, however, he managed to pass his students' examination in 1829 and he could now devote himself to the art of writing, which he had already, during the years of hardship, practised in secret.

He began as a lyrical and humorous poet. "The Dying Child" which was printed anonymously in 1827 had gained him a certain fame. The humorous story "Walking tour from Holmens Canal to Østpynten of Amager" made a name for him.

During one of his visits to Funen in 1830, he fell in love with the daughter of a rich merchant, Riborg Voigt, but she was already engaged. The outcome of this unhappy love affair was a collection of love poems, which in beauty are comparable with the finest in Danish literature. To console himself, he went in 1831 on his first trip abroad—to Northern Germany—which he describes in the book "Rambles in the Hartz Mountains". This first travel book revealed the rare powers of observation which were characteristic of all his later work.

So he started on the course which he was to follow throughout his life. A new era in his life was his journey to Italy 1833—34, which bore fruit in the book "The Improvisatore". This was translated into German and English which introduced him to a European public. The book was published in 1835, and the same year the first fairy-tales came out, but Hans Andersen himself regarded these as a mere bagatelle. He thought that the novel was the literary form which best suited him, and in the following years he produced a number of works which have now faded in the light of his fairy-tales, but they have a vigour all their own and they are filled with vivid scenes from his life and travels.

He never lost interest in the theatre. He revised the works of foreign authors, was successful in getting several accepted for performance at the Royal Theatre, wrote original plays, some of them melodramatic and of little worth, others—in which he adopted a popular tone and cast over them the brilliance of his make-believe—won favour among his contemporaries.

The fairy-tale, however, came to be the crowning glory of his work. Every year a small booklet of these stories was published, each perfect in form and content—superb masterpieces, which have made his name famed far beyond his native land.

It is said that the story of "The Ugly Duckling" is the life-story of Hans Andersen. With equal truth it can be said that the story "The Fir Tree" expresses the steady yearning after change which lay deep-seated in the soul of Hans Andersen.

Hans Andersen was never married. He was infatuated by Jonas Collin's daughter Louise. He was passionately in love with the great Swedish singer, Jenny Lind, whom he met in the 'forties at Copenhagen and in Berlin, but he never had a home except such as he found among his many good friends, first and foremost in the home of the Collin family. It was this home he sought with his joys and sorrows, and here he was looked upon as one of the family.

In Hans Andersen's Museum in Odense, we can see his travelling equipment, his bag, walking-stick and umbrella. These are symbolic of him. Travel was a vital necessity to him—seeking contact with other people in his native land and abroad.

From the middle of the 'thirties, he was a regular and welcome guest at Danish castles and manor-houses, where his stories were listened to with joy, and where he himself delighted in the beautiful surroundings and gathered inspiration for his writings. These sojourns were interrupted by his many journeys abroad, which, all in all, occupied about

29

nine years of his life. These journeys also brought him into easy and familiar contact with important personalities.

He often went to Germany, where he received great hospitality at the Royal Courts particularly at Weimar. He went to England in 1847 and 1857, when he made friends with Charles Dickens. In fact, he went to all countries in Europe. Italy was his favourite country. He felt quite at home wandering in the streets of Rome, and rejoiced in the blue Mediterranean and the brilliant sunshine. He had friends in Switzerland and was impressed by the magnificent scenery to which he gives expression in the story "The Ice Maiden". In 1840—41, he made the long journey to Greece and Turkey and reproduced his experiences in the breezy and delightful travel tale "A Poet's Bazaar". Spain, Portugal, Belgium and Holland, Sweden and Norway he visited once or more times. "To travel is to live" was one of his favourite sayings. He made notes of his impressions, drew sketches of the landscape and houses he saw, all with the intention of letting them settle down in his mind, to be reproduced one day, in his writings.

In the winter, when he was back home again in Copenhagen, he had to keep the connections he had made, and wrote letters to his friends. He wrote innumerable letters as rich and as entertaining as his stories, and they provide the best sources of information about his life.

Hans Andersen had a very sensitive nature. He took criticism very badly and suffered from a sense of bitterness when Danish critics, quite justly, raised objections to his dramatic works and found fault with his novels. It was some time before he understood that it was his fairy-tales that raised him above contemporary writers. Yet he was deeply touched and warmed in spirit when he found acknowledgement. He felt that his talent was more appreciated abroad, and that there they were less inclined to notice his short-comings.

The truth is, however, that his native land shed its appreciation on him in great measure. He enjoyed the favour and grace of the

Royal Family, he was honoured with titles and orders, and, as the years passed, his bitterness gave way to a profound feeling of fellowship with his native land, a feeling which matured to still greater fullness after Denmark's defeat in the war with Germany in 1864. In 1867 he was honoured with the Freedom of the City of his native town. Odense was illuminated, a torchlight procession was made for him, and then he felt how wonderfully God had guided him; that his life, indeed, was as a fairy-tale, rich and happy.

The last years of his life were marked by increasing illness, and only with difficulty could he go on his travels. He had, in Copenhagen, become closely attached to a wholesale merchant, M. G. Melchior, whose wife cared tenderly for him and in Melchior's home he died on the 4th August, 1875.

Other writers have, during their lifetime, attained similar renown, but the works of few authors live beyond the period of their creation. Hans Andersen's stories have done this. They were written for children, but it was Andersen's hope that their parents would also listen, and several of his stories are more for grown-ups than for children—for only the mature can understand the depth of these writings. Three-quarters of a century after his death, the name of Hans Christian Andersen shines among the most illustrious names of world literature, and his stories remain just as fresh and vigorous, for they are concerned with the emotions of mankind throughout the ages and are thus raised above the limitations of Time and Place.

Svend Larsen

THE TINDER-BOX

Left, right! Left, right! ... Down the country-road came a soldier marching. Left, right! Left, right! ... He had his knapsack on his back and a sword at his side, for he had been at the war, and now he was on his way home. But then he met an old witch on the road. Oh! she was ugly—her lower lip hung right down on her chest. "Good evening, soldier," she said, "what a nice sword you've got, and what a big knapsack! You're a proper soldier! Now I'll show you how to get as much money as you want!" "Thank you very much, old dame!" said the soldier.

"Do you see that big tree over there?" said the witch, pointing to a tree near by. "It's quite hollow inside. Now, you must climb right up it, and then you'll see a hole; slip through this, and you'll come deep down into the tree. I will tie a rope round your waist, so that I can haul you up again, as soon as you give me a shout."

"But what am I to do down in the tree?" asked the soldier.

"Fetch money!" answered the witch. "For, mind you, when you get down to the bottom of the tree, you will find yourself in a large passage. It's quite light there, because hundreds of lamps are burning there. Next, you will see three doors; you can open them all right, for the key's in the lock. If you go into the first room, you will see in the middle of the floor a big chest, with a dog sitting on it which has got eyes as big as tea-cups; but never you mind about that! I'll give you my blue-check apron, and you can spread it out on the floor. Then go along quickly and lift

36

off the dog and put it on my apron; open the lid of the chest and take just as many pennies as you like. They are all copper, but if you would rather have silver, then you must go into the next room. There sits a dog with eyes as large as mill-wheels, but never you mind about that! Put the dog down on my apron, and help yourself to the money! And yet, if it's gold you want, you can get that too—as much as ever you can carry—if only you go into the third room. But this time the dog which is sitting on the money-chest has two eyes each one as big as the Round Tower ... Something like a dog, I can tell you! But never you mind a bit about that! Just put the dog down on my apron, and then it won't do you any harm, and you can take as much gold out of the chest as you like."

"That doesn't sound at all bad", said the soldier. "But tell me, old witch, what am I to give you? Because I expect you'll be wanting your share!"

"No," said the witch, "not a single penny will I take. You've simply got to bring me an old tinder-box that my grandmother forgot, when she was last down there."

"Oh, come on, then! let me get that rope round my middle!" said the soldier.

"Here it is," said the witch, "and here's my blue-check apron.'

Then the soldier crawled up the tree, let himself down, plump! through the hole, and now he was standing, as the witch had said, down in the great passage where the hundreds of lamps were burning.

Then he unlocked the first door. Ugh! there sat the dog with eyes as big as tea-cups and glared at him.

"You are a nice chap, you are!" said the soldier. He put it down on the witch's apron and took just as many copper pennies as he could stuff into his pocket. Then he shut the chest, put the dog up again and went into the second room. Bless my soul! there sat the dog with eyes as big as mill-wheels.

"You shouldn't stare at me so!" said the soldier; "you'll strain your eyes." And then he put the dog down on the witch's apron; but when he saw such piles of silver in the chest, he threw away all the coppers he had got and filled up his pockets and his knapsack with nothing but silver. And now he went into the third room! ... Oh, but it was horrible! The dog in there had actually got two great eyes as big as the Round Tower, and they were going round and round in its head like wheels!

"Good evening!" said the soldier; and he touched his cap, because never in his life had he seen such a dog. But after he had looked at it for a bit, he thought to himself," Enough of that!" and went and lifted the dog down on to the floor and opened the chest—why, goodness gracious, what a lot of gold there was! There was enough for him to buy the whole of Copenhagen, all the sugar-pigs that the cake-women sell, and all the tin-soldiers and whips and rocking-horses in the world. Yes, yes, plenty of money in there—my word, there was!

So at once the soldier emptied out all the silver coins from his pockets and his knapsack and put in gold instead; yes, and he filled up everything with gold, his pockets, his knapsack, his cap and even his boots, so that he could hardly walk. Now he had got some money! He put the dog back on the chest, slammed the door, and then shouted up through the tree, "Hi, mother! haul me up again, will you?"

"Have you got the tinder-box?" asked the witch.

"Oh no! that's true, I had clean forgotten it", said the soldier; and he went straight back and fetched it. The witch hauled him up out of the tree, and there he was again, standing on the road with his pockets, boots, cap and knapsack bulging with money.

"What are you going to do with this tinder-box?" asked the soldier.

"That's no business of yours!" answered the witch. "You've got your money; now just give me my tinder-box!"

"Rubbish!" said the soldier. "Tell me at once what you want to do with it—or I'll have out my sword and cut your head off."

"No", said the witch.

So he cut off her head. . . . . There she lay!

40

But the soldier tied up all his money in her apron and made a bundle of it, to go on his back. He put the tinder-box in his pocket and went straight on into the town.

It was a fine town, and he put up at the finest inn. He ordered the very best rooms and the food he was most fond of; for, now that he had all that money, he was a rich man. The servant who had to clean his boots thought, well, this was a funny old pair of boots for such a rich gentleman to have; but he hadn't yet bought any new ones. The next day he went out and got some good boots and some really smart clothes. And now the soldier had become quite a fashionable gentleman, and they told him all about the sights of their town, and about their King, and what a pretty Princess his daughter was.

"Where is she to be seen?" asked the soldier.

"She just isn't to be seen", they all answered. "She lives in a big copper castle with lots of walls and towers all round it. No one but the king is allowed to go to her there, because a fortune-teller once said that she is to marry a common soldier, and the king doesn't like that at all."

"My word! I should like to see her", thought the soldier; but of course he couldn't possibly get leave to.

And now he lived a merry life.

He was always going to the theatre, or driving in the Park; and he gave away lots of money to the poor. That was very nice of him; you see, he remembered so well from the old days how awful it was to be absolutely penniless. But now he was rich and well-dressed, and so he made lots of friends who all said what a fine fellow he was—a real gentleman —and the soldier liked that very much. But as he was spending money every day and never getting any back, at last he had only got twopence left; and so he had to move from the fine rooms he had been living in and go and live in a little poky attic right under the roof. He had to clean his own boots and mend them with a darning-needle, and none of his friends ever came to see him, for there were such a lot of stairs to climb.

One evening, when it was quite dark and he

couldn't even buy himself a candle, he suddenly remembered that there was a little bit of candle left in the tinder-box that he had got for the old witch out of the hollow tree. So he fetched out the tinder-box and the bit of candle; but just as he was striking a light and the sparks flew up from the flint, the door sprang open, and the dog he had seen down in the tree with eyes as big as tea-cups stood before him and said "What are my lord's commands?"

"I say!" said the soldier. "This must be a queer sort of tinder-box, if I can get whatever I want like that." "Bring me some money", he said to the dog; then flick! and away it went, and flick! here it was back again, with a large bagful of pennies in its mouth.

And now the soldier realised what a splendid tinder-box it was. One stroke brought before him the dog which sat on the chest with the copper money; two strokes, the dog with the silver; and three strokes, the dog with the gold. The soldier lost no time in changing back into the fine rooms and the smart clothes, and of course all his friends remembered him again at once and were tremendously fond of him.

And then one day he thought to himself "There's something queer about this, that no one's allowed to see the Princess. She's supposed to be so very lovely, according to all these people; but what's the good of that, if she has to sit the whole time inside the copper castle, the one that has all those towers? Can't I possibly manage to see her somehow? Now then, where's my tinder-box?" So he struck a light and flick! there stood the dog with the eyes as big as tea-cups.

"Of course I know it's the middle of the night," said the soldier, "but all the same I would like to see the Princess, that I would! Just for half a jiffy!"

The dog was out of the door in a flash and, before the soldier had time to think about it, there was the dog again with the Princess lying asleep on his back; and she looked so lovely that anyone could see she was a real princess; and the soldier simply couldn't resist, he had to kiss her—he was a soldier all over.

44

Then the dog scuttled back again with the Princess, but in the morning, when the King and Queen were at breakfast, the Princess said she had had such a curious dream in the night, about a dog and a soldier. She had ridden on the dog's back, and the soldier had kissed her.

"That's a pretty tale, if you like!" said the Queen.

And so one of the old ladies-in-waiting was told to sit up the following night by the Princess's bed and see if it was really a dream or not.

The soldier did so long for another look at the pretty Princess; and so up came the dog by night and took her and dashed off at full speed. But the old lady-in-waiting put on her overboots and ran just as fast after them, and when she saw them disappear into a big house she thought to herself, "Now I know where it is", and chalked up a big cross on the door. Then she went home to bed, and the dog came back too with the Princess. But when it saw a cross had been chalked on the door where the soldier was living, the dog also took a bit of chalk and put a cross on every door in the town. That was a clever idea, because now, you see, the lady-in-waiting couldn't find the right door, as there were crosses on the whole lot of them.

Early in the morning the King and Queen, the old lady-in-waiting and all the Court officials sallied forth in order to see where it was the Princess had been.

"Here's the house!" said the King, when he saw the first door with a cross on it.

"No, it's there, darling!" said the Queen, catching sight of the second door with a cross on it.

"But here's another—and there's another!" they all kept saying. Whichever way they turned, there were crosses on the doors. So then they soon realised that it was no good searching any longer.

But the Queen, you know, was a very clever woman, who could do more than just drive out in a coach. She took her great golden scissors and cut up a large piece of silk and sewed the pieces together into a pretty little bag, which she filled with the finest buckwheat flour. She fastened the little bag to the Princess's back, and then she snipped a little hole in the bag, so as to sprinkle the flour wherever the Princess went.

At night, up came the dog once more, took the Princess on his back and ran off with her to the soldier, who loved her so dearly and did so wish he were a prince and could marry her.

The dog never noticed how the flour kept leaking out all the way from the castle to the soldier's window, where it ran up the wall with the Princess. The next morning it was quite plain to the King and Queen where their daughter had been going; so they took the soldier and put him in prison.

There he sat. Ugh! how dark and dreary his cell was! And, besides, they kept saying to him "To-morrow you're going to be hanged!" That didn't sound at all cheerful, and the worst of it was he had left his tinder-box at the inn. In the morning, through the iron bars of his little window, he watched people hurrying out of the town to see him hanged. He heard the drums and saw the soldiers marching past. Everyone was afoot. Among them was a cobbler's boy in leather apron and slippers; he was trotting along so fast that one of his slippers came off and flew right against the wall where the soldier sat peeping out between the iron bars.

"I say! you young cobbler, you don't need to hurry like that," the soldier said to him, "they can't begin without me. But look here —if you will kindly run along to where I've been living and fetch me my tinder-box, you shall have twopence for your trouble; but mind you get a move on!" The cobbler's boy was very glad to earn twopence, so he sprinted off for the tinder-box, brought it to the soldier, and—well, now listen to what happened!

Outside the town a high gallows had been built, and round about it stood the soldiers and thousands and thousands of people. The King and Queen sat on a beautiful throne opposite the judge and all his councillors.

Already the soldier had climbed the ladder; but just as they were going to put the rope round his neck he reminded them that, before being executed, a criminal always had the right to ask for one harmless favour. He said he would so like to smoke a pipe of tobacco —after all, it would be the last pipe he could smoke in this world.

Now, the King didn't like to say no to that; so the soldier took his tinder-box and struck a light—one, two, three!—and there stood all three dogs: the one with eyes as big as tea-cups, the one with eyes like mill-wheels, and the one which had eyes as big as the Round Tower.

"Save me now from being hanged!" said the soldier; and then the dogs flew at the judges and all the councillors, and seized some by their legs and others by their noses, and tossed them so high into the air that when they came down they were dashed to pieces.

"I won't be tossed!" said the King; but the biggest dog picked them both up, King and Queen, and sent them hurtling after the others. Then the soldiers got frightened, and the people all shouted out "Soldier boy, you shall be our King and have the pretty Princess". And they put the soldier into the King's coach, and all three dogs went dancing in front of it and cried out "Hurrah!" And the boys whistled on their fingers, and the soldiers presented arms. The Princess came out of the copper castle and was made Queen, and how pleased she was! The wedding-feast lasted for a week, and the dogs sat at table with everyone else and kept rolling their great big eyes.

LITTLE CLAUS AND
BIG CLAUS

There were two men in one village, who both had the very same name; they **were** both called Claus. One of them owned four horses, the other only one; and, to tell them from each other, people called the man who had four horses Big Claus, and the man who had only one horse Little Claus. Now let us hear how these two got on; for this is a **true** story.

All through the week Little Claus **had** to plough for Big Claus and lend him his one horse; in return, Big Claus gave him the help of all his four horses, but only once **a week**,

1 4*

51

and that was on Sunday. My word! How
Little Claus did crack his whip over all five
horses! They were as good as his—for that
one day. The sun shone so pleasantly, and the
church-bells were all ringing for church; the
villagers went by in their Sunday best, with
their hymn-books under their arms, to hear
the parson preach, and when they looked at
Little Claus ploughing with five horses, he
was so delighted that he cracked his whip once
more and cried out: "Gee up, all my horses!"

"You mustn't say that," said Big Claus;
"there's only one horse, you know, which is
yours." But when some more people went
past on their way to church, Little Claus forgot that he wasn't to say that and cried out
again: "Gee up, all my horses!"

"Look here, will you kindly give over?"
said Big Claus. "The next time you say that,
I'll give your horse a clump on the head and
kill him on the spot; and that'll be good-bye
to him."

"I promise you I won't say it again", said
Little Claus. But when some more people went
by and they nodded good-morning to him, he

was so delighted and felt that it must look so smart for him to have five horses to plough his field with, that he cracked his whip and cried out: "Gee up, all my horses!"

"I'll gee up your horses for you!" said Big Claus, and he took the mallet for the tether-peg, and gave Little Claus's one horse such a clump on the forehead that it fell down stone dead.

"Oh, dear! Now I haven't a horse at all", said Little Claus and began to cry. By and by he flayed the dead horse and took the hide and gave it a thorough drying in the wind. Then he stuck it in a bag, which he threw over his shoulder, and went off to the next town to sell his horse-hide.

He had a long way to go, and it led through a big, gloomy wood. Presently a terrible storm got up, and he quite lost his way. It was evening before he could find it again, and he was much too far from the town or from home to be able to reach either before night fell.

Close to the road stood a large farmhouse; the windows had the shutters up outside, but yet a gleam of light showed over the top of them. "I daresay I can get leave to spend the night there", thought Little Claus and went up and knocked at the door.

The farmer's wife came and opened it; but when she heard what he wanted, she told him to be off, as her husband was not at home, and she didn't take in strangers.

"Oh, well, in that case I must find a bed out of doors", said Little Claus, and the farmer's wife shut the door in his face.

Near by was a big haystack, and between this and the house a little shed had been built, with a flat thatch roof to it.

"I can sleep up there", said Little Claus, catching sight of the roof; "that will be a lovely bed, and I shouldn't think the stork will fly down and bite my legs"; for a real live stork was standing up there on the roof, where it had its nest.

Little Claus now crawled up on to the shed, where he lay and wriggled himself to get really comfortable. The wooden shutters didn't quite cover the windows up at the top, and so he was able to see right into the room.

54

There was a large table laid with wine and roast meat and oh! such a delicious-looking fish. The farmer's wife and the parish clerk were sitting at table all by themselves; and she kept filling up his glass for him, and he kept helping himself to the fish—he was very fond of fish.

"If only I could get a taste of that!" thought Little Claus, craning out his neck towards the window. Heavens! What a gorgeous cake he could see in there! It was really a wonderful spread.

Then he heard someone riding along the road towards the house. It was the farmer himself, coming home.

Now, although he was an excellent man, the farmer had the strange failing that he never could bear the sight of a parish clerk; if he ever set eyes on a clerk, he flew into an absolute rage. And that was just why this clerk had called in to pass the time of day with the farmer's wife, when he knew that her husband was away from home; and the good woman set before him all the nicest things to eat that she could find. And now, when they heard the husband coming, they got so scared that the woman begged the clerk to creep into a big empty chest which stood over in the corner. So he climbed in, for he knew quite well that the poor man couldn't bear the sight of a parish clerk. The woman quickly hid away all the delicious food and wine inside her oven, because if her husband had seen it he would have been sure to ask what it all meant.

"Oh, dear!" sighed Little Claus up on the shed, when he saw all the food disappearing.

"Is that somebody up there?" asked the farmer, peering up at Little Claus. "What are you lying up there for? Much better come along o' me into the house!"

Little Claus then explained how he had lost his way and asked if he might stop the night.

"Why, certainly," said the farmer, "but first we must have a bit o' something to eat."

The farmer's wife gave them both a most friendly welcome, laid a long table and gave them a large bowl of porridge. The farmer was hungry, and he ate with a good appetite; but

Little Claus couldn't help thinking about the lovely roast meat, the fish and the cake which he knew were inside the oven.

Under the table, at his feet, he had placed his sack with the horse-hide in it; for we mustn't forget, it was the hide which he had brought away with him from home, in order to sell it in the town. He didn't care for the porridge at all; and so he trod on his bag, and the dry hide inside it gave out quite a loud squeak.

"'Sh!" said Little Claus to his sack; but at the same time he trod on it again, and it gave out a still louder squeak.

"Why, what ever have you got in that there bag?" asked the farmer.

"Oh, it's a wizard", said Little Claus. "He says that we shouldn't be eating porridge; he has conjured the whole oven full of meat and fish and cake."

"You don't say so!" said the farmer, and in a twinkling he opened the oven and saw all the delicious food which his wife had hidden away, though he thought himself that the wizard had conjured it there. His wife didn't dare say a word; she put the food straight on the table, and they both made a good meal off the fish and the meat and the cake. Presently Little Claus trod on his bag once more and made the hide squeak.

"What's he say now?" asked the farmer.

"He says", answered Little Claus, "that he has also conjured us three bottles of wine, and they're in the oven too." So the wife had to bring out the wine she had hidden, and the farmer drank and became quite merry; he felt he'd give anything to own a wizard like the one Little Claus had got in his bag.

"Can he also make the devil appear?" asked the farmer. "I should so like to see him, now that I'm feeling so cheerful."

"Certainly," said Little Claus, "my wizard can do whatever I like to ask him—can't you, old man?" and at the same time he trod on the bag so that it squeaked. "Did you hear him? He says, yes, of course he can; but the devil's so hideous that you'd better not see him."

"Oh, I'm not afeard. What d'you think he'll look like?"

58

"Well, you'll find he's the very image of a parish clerk."

"Ugh!" said the farmer, "that's hideous and no mistake! You know, I can't abear the sight of parish clerks; but never mind, I know it's the devil this time, so I reckon I'll put up with it for once. I'm full o' pluck just now— but don't let him come too near!"

"Now I'll ask my wizard", said Little Claus, treading on the bag and turning his ear to it.

"What's he say?"

"He says you may go up and open the chest which is standing over there in the corner, and you'll see the devil squatting inside; but mind you hold on to the lid, or he'll slip out."

"Come and help me hold it, then!" said the farmer, going across to the chest in which his wife had hidden the real clerk, who sat there trembling with fear.

The farmer raised the lid a little way and peeped in under it: "Ugh!" he shrieked and jumped back from the chest. "Yes, I saw him right enough; he looked the dead spit of our clerk—oh, it was horrible!"

They had to have a drink after that, and they went on drinking far into the night.

"You must sell me that wizard", said the farmer. "Ask what you like for him! I tell you what, I'll give you a whole bushel of money straight away."

"No", said Claus. "I can't do that. Just think of the profit I can make out of this wizard."

"Oh, but I'm fair crazy to have him", said the farmer, and he begged and pleaded till at last Little Claus said yes. "You've been very kind and given me a good night's lodging, so it doesn't make much odds. You shall have the wizard for a bushel of money, but full measure, mind you!"

"Right you are!" said the farmer. "But you must take that there chest with you; I won't have it another hour in the place—he may be in there yet, for all we can tell."

Little Claus gave the farmer his sack with the dry hide in it, and got a whole bushel of money, full measure, in exchange. What's more, the farmer gave him a large barrow on which to wheel away the chest and the money.

"Good-bye!" said Little Claus, and off he
went trundling his money and the great chest
with the clerk still in it.

On the other side of the wood ran a deep
river, where the current was so strong that you

could hardly swim against it. A big bridge had lately been built across it, and Little Claus halted when he got to the middle and said out aloud, so that the clerk in the chest could hear him: "Hang it all! What ever am I to do with this stupid chest? It's so heavy, you'd think it was full of stones. I'm sick and tired of wheeling it, so I'll just tip it into the river. Then, if it sails home to me, very good; and if it doesn't—well, it can't be helped."

Then he took hold of the chest by one of the handles and tilted it a bit, as though he meant to hurl it down into the water.

"Stop! Stop!" shouted the clerk from inside the chest. "Let me out! Oh, do let me out!"

"Good gracious!" said Little Claus and pretended to be frightened. "He's still inside! I must push him into the river at once, and then he'll drown!"

"No! No!" shouted the clerk. "I'll give you a whole bushel of money, if you'll let me out."

"Ah, that's another story", said Little Claus and opened the chest. The clerk quickly crept out, pushed the empty chest into the water and went to his home, where Little Claus was given a whole bushel of money. He had already got one out of the farmer, so there he was now with his wheelbarrow chock-full of money.

"There! I got rather a good price for that horse!" he said to himself, when he came home to his own room and turned out all the money in a big heap on the floor. "Big Claus will be very annoyed when he hears how rich I've become out of my one horse; but all the same I won't tell him straight away."

Presently he sent a boy along to Big Claus to borrow a bushel measure.

"I wonder what he wants that for?" thought Big Claus, and he smeared the bottom with tar, so that a little of whatever was measured might stick to it; and, sure enough, when the measure came back, there were three new silver florins sticking to it.

"Hullo, what's this?" said Big Claus, and ran straight off to Little Claus. "Where did you get all this money from?"

"Oh, that was for my horse-hide that I sold yesterday."

"That's a wonderful good price!" said Big Claus; and he ran home, took an axe and gave all his four horses a clump on the forehead. Then he stripped off the hides and trundled them away into the town.

"Hides! Hides! Who'll buy my hides?" he shouted through the streets.

All the shoemakers and tanners came running up and asking how much he wanted for them.

"A bushel of money apiece!" said Big Claus.

"Are you mad?" they all asked him. "Do you suppose we keep money in bushels?"

"Hides! Hides! Who'll buy my hides?" he shouted again; but to everyone who asked him the price he answered: "A bushel of money."

"He's trying to make fools of us", they all said; and then the shoemakers took their straps and the tanners their leather aprons and began to give Big Claus a good beating

"Hides! Hides!" they mocked at him, "we'll give you a hide that'll bleed like a pig! Out of the town with him!" they shouted; and

Big Claus had to bolt for his life—he'd never had such a drubbing.

"All right!" he said, when he got home. "Little Claus shall pay for this. I'll beat his brains out."

But at Little Claus's home his old grandmother had just died. It's true she had always been very cross and unkind to him; still, he was very much grieved and took the dead woman and laid her in his own warm bed, to see if he couldn't bring her to life again. She was to lie there all night, while he himself would sit over in the corner and sleep on a chair; it wouldn't be the first time he had done that.

During the night, as he was sitting there, the door opened and Big Claus came in with an axe. He knew quite well where Little Claus's bed was, so he went straight up to it, and, thinking the dead grandmother was Little Claus, gave her a great clump on the forehead.

"There now!" he said, "you're not going to make a fool of me again"; and he went back home.

"What a very wicked man!" said Little

Claus to himself. "It's clear that he meant to kill me. Anyhow, it's a good thing for the old dame that she was dead already, otherwise he would have taken her life."

And now he dressed up the old grandmother in her Sunday clothes, borrowed a horse from his neighbour, harnessed it to the cart and set up the old grandmother in the back seat, so that she couldn't fall out when he drove faster, and away they bowled through the woods. By sunrise they were outside a large inn, where Little Claus drew up and went inside to get something to eat.

The landlord of the inn had plenty of money and was a very kind man too; but he was hot-tempered, as if he were full of pepper and snuff.

"Good morning!" he said to Little Claus. "You're out early to-day in your best clothes."

"Yes," said Little Claus, "I'm off to town with my old grandmother. She's sitting out in the cart; I can't get her to come in here. Will you take her a large glass of honey-wine? But you must speak rather loud, for she's a bit deaf."

"Right you are!" said the landlord and poured out a large glass of honey-wine, which he took out with him to the dead grandmother who was propped up in the cart.

"Here's a glass of honey-wine from your son, lady", said the landlord. But the dead woman never said a word nor moved a muscle.

"Can't you hear?" cried the landlord at the top of his voice; "here's a glass of honey-wine from your son!"

Once more he shouted it out, and yet again after that; but as she never stirred, he lost his temper and threw the glass right into her face, so that the wine ran down over her nose and she toppled over backwards into the cart; for she was only propped up and not fastened in.

"Hi! What's this?" cried Little Claus, rushing out and seizing the landlord by the throat. "You've been and killed my grandmother! Just look, there's a big hole in her forehead!"

"Oh, dear! That's a bit of bad luck!" cried the landlord, wringing his hands. "That all comes of my hot temper. Dear, kind Little Claus, I'll give you a whole bushel of money and bury your grandmother as if she was my own, if only you'll not say a word. Otherwise they'll cut off my head, and that is so disagreeable!"

So Little Claus got a whole bushel of money, and the landlord buried his old grandmother as if she had been his own.

As soon as Little Claus got back home with all his money, he sent his boy along to Big Claus to ask if he'd lend him a bushel measure.

"Hullo, what's this?" said Big Claus. "Didn't I kill him? I really must see about this myself." And he went over to Little Claus with the measure.

"Why, where ever have you got all this money from?" he asked, and my goodness! how he opened his eyes when he saw all the fresh money that had come in.

"It was my grandmother you killed, not me", said Little Claus. "It's she I've just sold and got a bushel of money for."

"That's a wonderful good price", said Big Claus and hurried home, took an axe and quickly killed his old grandmother. Then he placed her in the cart, drove into the town where the doctor lived, and asked if he wanted to buy a dead body.

"Whose is it and where did you get it?" asked the doctor.

"It's my old grandmother", said Big Claus. "I killed her to get a bushel of money."

"Good gracious!" said the doctor, "you don't know what you're saying. Don't go babbling like that, or you may lose your head!" And then he told him frankly what a dreadfully wicked thing he had done, and what a bad man he was, and that he ought to be punished. This made Big Claus so frightened that he rushed straight out of the surgery into the cart, whipped up the horses and made for home. But the doctor and the rest of them thought he was mad, and so they left him to drive where he liked.

"You shall pay for this!" said Big Claus, once he was out on the high-road. "Yes, you shall certainly pay for this, Little Claus!" And, as soon as he got home, he took the biggest sack he could find, went along to Little Claus and said: "You've been and fooled me again! First, I killed my horses, and then my old grandmother. It was your fault both times, but you shan't fool me any more!" And he caught hold of Little Claus by the waist, thrust him into the sack, slung him over his shoulder and called out to him: "Now I'm going to take you out and drown you!"

There was some distance to go before he came to the river, and Little Claus was no light weight to carry. The road went past the church; and the sound of the organ playing and the people singing was so beautiful that Big Claus put down his sack, with Little Claus inside it, near by the church door and thought it would be nice to go in and listen to a hymn first before he went any further. Little Claus couldn't possibly get out, and everybody was in church; so in he went.

"Oh, dear! Oh, dear!" sighed Little Claus inside the sack. He wriggled and wriggled, but he couldn't possibly manage to get the string unfastened. Just then an old cattle-drover came up. His hair was as white as chalk, and he leaned on a big stick, as he drove a whole herd of cows and bullocks in front of him; these ran up to the sack, in which Little Claus was sitting, and over-turned it.

"Oh, dear!" sighed Little Claus, "I'm so young to go to heaven!"

"And poor me!" said the drover, "I'm so old and I can't get there!"

"Open the sack!" called out Little Claus. "Crawl in here instead of me, and you'll soon get to heaven!"

"Ah! I'd give anything for that," said the drover, and he unfastened the sack for Little Claus, who jumped out at once.

"You'll mind the cattle, won't you?" said the old man, as he crawled into the bag. Little Claus tied it up and went on his way with all the cows and bullocks.

Soon after, Big Claus came out of church and put the sack over his shoulder again. Sure enough, he noticed that it seemed lighter; for the old drover wasn't more than half the weight of Little Claus. "How light he's become! No doubt it's because I listened to a hymn." Then off he went to the river, which was a deep one. and threw the sack with the old drover inside it right out into the stream

71

and shouted after him, thinking of course that it was Little Claus: "There now! You shan't fool me any more!"

Then he turned homeward, but when he came to the cross-roads he met Little Claus driving off with all his cattle.

"Hullo, what's this?" said Big Claus, "didn't I drown you?'

"Yes, you did", said Little Claus. "You threw me into the river barely half an hour ago."

"But where did you get all those fine cattle from?" asked Big Claus.

"They're sea-cattle", said Little Claus. "I must tell you the whole story; and, by the by, thank you so much for drowning me. I'm in luck's way now; I'm really rich, I can tell you! ...

"I was very frightened, as I lay inside the sack with the wind whistling round my ears, when you threw me down off the bridge into the cold water. I sank straight to the bottom, but I didn't hurt myself, because down there grows the finest, softest grass. As I came down on this, the bag at once opened, and the most lovely girl dressed in pure white, with a green garland on her wet hair, took my hand and said: 'Is that you, Little Claus? Here are a few cattle for you to go on with. About four miles further up the road there's another drove of them, which I'll make you a present of'. ...

"Then I could see that the river was a great high-road for the sea-people. Down there at the bottom they walked and drove straight out of the sea, and then right away inland to where the river rises. It was delightful down there—what with flowers and the freshest grass, and fishes swimming about in the water and darting past my ears as birds do in the air up here. What fine folk there were, and what cattle to be met with along the hedges and ditches!"

"But why have you come up to us again in such a hurry?" asked Big Claus. "I wouldn't have done that, if it was so beautiful down there."

"Ah, but that's just where I've been rather cunning", said Little Claus. "You remember I told you what the sea-maiden said—that about four miles further up the road (and by the road she means of course the river, as she can't go anywhere else) there's another drove of cattle waiting for me. Well, I know how the river keeps winding in and out; it would be a very roundabout way, you know. So, if you can do it, it's much shorter to come up on land and drive straight across to the river again. You see, I save almost half the distance that way and get to my sea-cattle more quickly."

"Oh, what a lucky man you are!" said Big Claus. "Do you think I shall get some sea-cattle too, if I go down to the bottom of the river?"

"I should just think you would!" said Little Claus; "but I can't carry you as far as the river in the sack, you're too heavy. If you will go there yourself and then crawl into the bag, I'll throw you into the water with the greatest of pleasure."

"Thanks very much," said Big Claus, "but if I don't find any sea-cattle when I get down there, I'll give you such a beating, I can tell you!"

"Oh, no; don't be so cruel!" So they went off to the river. The cattle were thirsty and,

when they saw the water, they trotted off as fast as they could so as to get down and have a drink.

"Look what a hurry they're in", said Little Claus. "They're longing to get down to the bottom again."

"Yes, but help me first", said Big Claus, "or you'll get your beating!" And then he crawled into the big sack, which had been lying across the back of one of the herd. "Better put a stone in, or else I'm afraid I mayn't sink", said Big Claus.

"I expect you'll sink all right", said Little

Claus. Still, he put a big stone in the sack, tied the string tight and then gave it a good push —plomp!—there was Big Claus out in the river, and he sank straight to the bottom.

"I'm afraid he won't find his cattle", said Little Claus—and drove off home with what he had.

THE PRINCESS AND
THE PEA

Once upon a time there was a Prince, who wanted to have a Princess of his own, but she must be a proper Princess. So he travelled all over the world in order to find such a one, but every time there was something wrong. There were plenty of Princesses, but he could never quite make out if they were real Princesses; there was always something that wasn't quite right. So he came back home and was very much upset, because he did so long for a real Princess.

One evening a terrible storm blew up. There was lightning and thunder, the rain came pouring down—it was something dreadful! All at once there was a knock at the city gate, and the old King went out to open it.

It was a Princess standing outside. But goodness! what a sight she was with the rain and the weather! The water was running all down her hair and her clothes, and in at the tip of her shoes and out again at the heels; and yet she declared she was a real Princess.

"Well, we shall soon see about that!" thought the old Queen. She didn't say anything, but she went into the bedroom, took off all the bedclothes and placed a pea on the bottom of the bed; then she took twenty mattresses and laid them on top of the pea, and then again twenty of the softest feather-beds on top of the mattresses. That's where the Princess had to sleep for the night.

In the morning they asked her how she had slept. "Oh, dreadfully badly!" said the Princess. "I hardly had a wink of sleep all night! Goodness knows what there was in the bed! I was lying on something so hard that I'm simply black and blue all over. It's perfectly dreadful!"

So then of course they could see that she really was a Princess, because she had felt the pea right through the twenty mattresses and the twenty feather-beds. Nobody but a real Princess could have such a tender skin as that.

And so the Prince took her to wife, because now he knew that he had a proper Princess. And the pea was sent to the museum, where it is still to be seen, unless someone has taken it.

There, that's something like a story, isn't it?

LITTLE IDA'S FLOWERS

My poor flowers are quite dead!" said little Ida. "Yesterday evening they were so pretty, and now their leaves are all drooping. Why is it?" she asked of the student who was sitting on the sofa. She was very fond of him, because he knew the most lovely stories and could cut out such amusing pictures— hearts with little dancing ladies inside them, flowers, and great castles with doors that opened. He was a very jolly student.

"Why do the flowers look so unwell today?" she asked once more, pointing to a whole nosegay that was quite withered.

"Ah! don't you know what's the matter with them?" said the student. "The flowers were at a dance last night, that's why they're hanging their heads."

"But flowers can't dance!" said little Ida.

"Can't they!" said the student. "When it's dark and we are all asleep, they go hopping round quite gaily; almost every night in the year they have a dance."

"Are children allowed to join in?"

"Certainly", said the student; "tiny little daisies are allowed to, and lilies-of-the-valley."

"Where do the loveliest flowers dance?" asked little Ida.

"You've often been out of town, haven't you, to look at all the beautiful flowers in the garden of the great castle where the King lives in summer? Then you must have seen the swans which swim up to you, when you offer them bread-crumbs. There are wonderful dances out there, I can tell you!"

"I was out in that garden yesterday with my mother", said Ida, "but the leaves were all off the trees, and there wasn't a single flower left. Where are they? I saw so many there last summer."

"They are inside the castle", said the student. "You see, directly the King and all his Court come back to town, the flowers at once run up from the garden into the castle and make merry. You should just see them! The two finest roses go and sit on the throne— they are King and Queen. All the red cockscombs line up on both sides and bow—they are gentlemen-in-waiting. Then come all the prettiest flowers, and there is a grand ball. The blue violets are young naval cadets, and they dance with the hyacinths and crocuses, whom they call Miss. The tulips and the large yellow lilies are old dowagers, who keep an eye on the dancing and see that everybody behaves."

"But look here", asked little Ida, "isn't there anyone to scold the flowers for dancing at the King's castle?"

"Nobody really knows what's going on"; said the student. "Sometimes, it's true, the old castle-steward, who is on watch there, comes along at night with his great bunch of

82

keys; but as soon as the flowers hear the keys rattle, they don't make a sound, but hide behind the long curtains and poke their heads out. 'I can smell flowers in here', says the old steward, but he can't see them."

"What fun!" said little Ida, clapping her hands. "But shouldn't I be able to see the flowers either?"

"Oh, yes!" said the student. "You must just remember, next time you go out there, to peep in at the windows. You'll be sure to see the flowers. I did to-day. I saw a long yellow daffodil lolling on the sofa and pretending she was a maid-of-honour."

"Can the flowers in the Botanical Garden go out there too? Can they go all that way?"

"Ra-ther!" said the student, "because they can fly, if they want to. You've seen lots of pretty butterflies, haven't you? Red ones and white ones and yellow ones—they almost look like flowers, don't they? They were flowers once, but then they jumped off their stalks high into the air and kept flapping their petals as if they were little wings, and away they flew. And as they behaved nicely, they got leave to fly about by day as well—they didn't have to go back and sit still on their stalks — and so at last their petals grew into real wings. You've seen that, of course, yourself. All the same, it's quite possible that the flowers at the Botanical Garden have never been out to the King's castle and that they have no idea of the fun that goes on there at night. Well, now I'm going to tell you something which will quite astonish the Professor of Botany who lives close by—you know him, don't you? When you go into his garden, you're to tell one of the flowers that there's a grand ball out at the castle. This flower will be sure to pass the news on to the others, and so they will all fly away. Then, if the Professor walks out into his garden, there won't be a single flower left and he won't have the slightest idea what has become of them."

"But how can the flowers tell the others about the ball? Flowers can't talk, can they?"

"No, not exactly", answered the student; "but they do it by signs. Surely you've noticed them, when it's a bit windy—how the flowers keep nodding and fluttering their green leaves; that means as much to them as if they talked."

"Does the Professor understand their signs, then?" asked Ida.

"I should just think he does! Why, one morning he went into his garden and saw a great stinging-nettle making signs with its leaves to a lovely red carnation; it was saying, 'You are so attractive, and I am so fond of you!' But the Professor can't bear that sort of thing, and he at once rapped the stinging-nettle over its leaves—for they are its fingers—but in doing this he stung himself and, ever since, he has always been afraid to touch a stinging-nettle."

"What fun!" said little Ida, with a laugh.

"Fancy filling a child's head with such rubbish!" said the grumpy old Councillor, who had come to pay a visit and was sitting on the sofa. He never could bear the student and always got cross when he saw him cutting out those comic figures which were so amusing—sometimes it was a man hanging from a gibbet, with a heart in his hand because he

85

was a stealer of hearts; sometimes an old witch riding on a broomstick, with her husband perched on the bridge of her nose. The Councillor couldn't bear that sort of thing, and he always used to say just what he said now: "What rubbish to put into a child's head! All stuff and nonsense!"

But little Ida was most amused at what the student had said about her flowers, and she thought about it for a long time. The flowers drooped their heads because they were tired out from dancing all night. No mistake about it, they were ill. So she took them along to her other playthings, which stood on a nice little table where she kept all her treasures in a drawer. Her doll, Sophie, lay sleeping in her little bed, but Ida said to her: "You really must get up, Sophie, and be content with sleeping in the drawer to-night. The poor flowers are ill, and so they must sleep in your bed, then perhaps they will get well again." She picked up the doll, which looked cross and never said a word, because it was annoyed at having to give up its bed.

Ida laid the flowers in the doll's bed, tucked

them well up and told them to lie quite still while she made them some tea; then they would be well enough to get up next morning. She pulled the curtains close round the little bed, so that the sun shouldn't shine into their eyes.

All that evening she couldn't stop thinking about what the student had told her and, now that it was time to go to bed herself, she had first to take a peep behind the curtains drawn across the window, where her mother's beautiful flowers were standing. They were hyacinths and tulips, and she whispered to them quite softly: "I know perfectly well where you're going to-night!" But the flowers pretended they didn't understand a word, and they never stirred a leaf; but little Ida knew perfectly well what they were up to.

When she had got into bed, she lay for a long time thinking how jolly it would be to see the beautiful flowers dancing out there at the King's castle. "I wonder if my flowers really went too." But then she fell asleep. In the middle of the night she woke up again; she had been dreaming about the flowers and the student whom the Councillor scolded because he filled her head with rubbish. There wasn't a sound in the bedroom where Ida lay, the night-light was quietly burning on the table, and her father and mother were asleep.

"I wonder if my flowers are still lying in Sophie's bed", she said to herself; "I should like to know!" She sat up in bed and looked over at the door, which stood ajar. In there lay the flowers and all her playthings. She listened carefully, and then it was just as though she heard a piano being played in the next room, but quite softly and more beautifully than she had ever heard before.

"That must be the flowers all dancing in there!" she said. "Oh dear, how I should like to see them!" But she didn't dare get up for fear of waking her father and mother. "If only they would come in here!" she said. But the flowers never came, and the music went on playing so beautifully that she couldn't stay where she was any longer, it was too lovely. She crept out of her little bed and went softly across to the door and peeped into the next room. Oh, it was really too amusing, what she saw in there.

There was no night-light of any sort, but all the same it wasn't a bit dark, for the moon was shining through the window on to the middle of the floor—it was almost as clear as daylight. All the hyacinths and tulips were standing on the floor in two long rows; there wasn't one left in the window, where the pots stood empty. Down on the floor all the flowers were dancing round so nicely together, actually doing the Grand Chain, and holding each other by their long green leaves as they swung round. But over at the piano sat a tall yellow lily, which little Ida was sure she had seen last summer; for she remembered the student saying: "Isn't it like Miss Lena!" Everybody had laughed at him, but now Ida, too, thought that the long yellow flower really was like Miss Lena. It had just the same way of sitting at the piano, and of turning its sallow oval face first to one side and then to the other, while it nodded time to the pretty music. Nobody noticed little Ida.

Next she saw a big blue crocus jump on to

the middle of the table, where her playthings were lying, and go straight up to the doll's bed and pull aside the curtains. There lay the sick flowers; but they sat up at once and nodded to the others that they would gladly come down and join in the dancing. The old chimney-sweep, whose lower lip had broken off, stood up and bowed to the dainty flowers, which didn't look in the least ill, but jumped down among the others and enjoyed themselves like anything.

Suddenly something seemed to fall down off the table. Ida saw that it was the teaser she had been given for the carnival; it had jumped down, because it felt it was really one of the flowers. It certainly looked fine with its paper streamers, and at the top of it was a little wax doll, wearing just such a wide-awake hat as the Councillor went about in. The teaser, on its three red wooden legs, hopped right in among the flowers and stamped away like anything, for it was dancing the mazurka, and that's a dance the other flowers couldn't manage, because they were too light to stamp properly.

90

All at once the wax doll at the end of the teaser seemed to grow bigger and taller; it whirled round above its own paper flowers and shouted at the top of its voice: "What rubbish to put into a child's head! All stuff and nonsense!" The wax doll was the very image of the Councillor, all sallow and grumpy, in his wide-awake hat, but the teaser's paper flowers kept curling round his thin legs, and then he shrank together and became a little shrimp of a wax doll again. It was such fun to watch, and little Ida couldn't help laughing. The teaser went on dancing and the Councillor had to dance as well. It made no difference whether he grew large and lanky or remained the little yellow wax doll in the big black hat, he had to keep on dancing—till at last the other flowers, and especially those which had been lying in the doll's bed, begged him off, and the teaser stopped. At the same moment there was a loud knocking inside the drawer, where Ida's doll, Sophie, was lying among a lot of other playthings. The chimney-sweep ran along to the edge of the table and, lying full length on

91

his stomach, he managed to work the drawer a little way open. Sophie sat up and looked around her in utter astonishment. "Why, there's a dance going on here!" she said. "Why didn't anyone tell me about it?"

"Will you dance with me?" said the chimney-sweep.

"I should think so! You're a fine one to dance with!"—and she turned her back on him. Then she sat down on the drawer, thinking that one of the flowers would be sure to come and ask her for a dance; but nobody came. She kept coughing—ahem! ahem!—it made no difference, not a soul came up to her. So the chimney-sweep danced by himself, and he didn't get on at all badly either.

And now, as none of the flowers seemed to notice Sophie, she let herself fall down, plump! on to the floor. It was a terrific thud. All the flowers came running up and stood round her, asking if she had hurt herself. They all behaved so nicely to her, especially the flowers who had been lying in her bed; but she hadn't hurt herself in the slightest, and all Ida's flowers said: "Thank you for the lovely bed" and made a great fuss of her and took her along to the moonlight in the middle of the floor and danced with her, while the other flowers made a ring round them. Sophie was delighted, and told them they were quite welcome to keep her bed, as she didn't a bit mind sleeping in the drawer.

But the flowers answered: "Thank you very, very much, but we can't live very long; we've only got till to-morrow. But please tell little Ida to bury us out in the garden where the canary was buried; then we shall sprout up again next summer and be far prettier."

"Oh, no! You mustn't die", said Sophie, as she kissed the flowers. At the same moment the drawing-room door opened, and a whole throng of beautiful flowers came dancing in. Ida couldn't make out where they came from, but of course they were all the flowers which had come in from the King's castle. Two lovely roses, wearing little crowns of gold, led the way; they were the King and Queen. Next came the most charming stocks and carnations, bowing in every direction. There was a band playing, too—great poppies and peonies blowing away on pea-shells till they were purple in the face, and harebells and little white snowdrops tinkling along as if they had real bells. It was such funny music. After that came a lot of other flowers, and they all danced together—the blue violets and the red daisies, the ox-eyes and the lilies-of-the-valley. And it was pretty to see how the flowers all kissed each other. At last they said good-night to one another, and little Ida also crept away to bed, where she dreamt of all she had seen.

When she got up next morning, she went straight along to the little table, to see if the flowers were still there. She drew back the curtains of the little bed—yes, there they all lay together; but they were quite withered, much more than they were yesterday. Sophie was still in the drawer where Ida had put her; she was looking very sleepy.

"Do you remember what you were to tell me?" asked little Ida; but Sophie looked very stupid and didn't say a word.

"You're very naughty", said Ida, "and yet they all danced with you." Then she took a

little **cardboard** box, which had a pretty design of birds on it, and taking off the lid she placed the dead flowers inside it. 'There's a nice coffin for you", she said, "and later on, when my Norwegian cousins arrive, they will help me to bury you out in the garden, so that you can sprout up again next summer and become still prettier."

The Norwegian cousins were two lively boys called Jonas and Adolph, whose father had just given them new bows and arrows, and they brought these with them to show to Ida. She told them all about the poor dead flowers, and they got leave to bury them. The two boys walked in front with the bows over their shoulders, and little Ida followed with the dead flowers in the pretty box. Out in the garden they dug a small grave. Ida first kissed the flowers, and then she placed them, box and all, in the earth; and, as they hadn't any guns or cannons, Adolph and Jonas fired a salute over the grave with their bows and arrows.

THUMBELINA

There was once a woman who did so want to have a wee child of her own, but she had no idea where she was to get it from. So she went off to an old witch and said to her, "I would so dearly like to have a little child. Do please tell me where I can find one."

"Oh, that!" said the witch, "Nothing easier. Take this barleycorn—mind you, it's not the kind that grows out in the fields or that the fowls are fed with. Put it in a flower-pot, and see what happens!"

"Thank you very much", said the woman, giving the witch a shilling. She went straight home and planted the barleycorn, and in no time there came up a lovely great flower which looked just like a tulip, only the petals were shut tight as though it were still in bud.

"It *is* a pretty flower", said the woman, and she gave the lovely red and yellow petals a kiss; but directly she kissed it, the flower burst open with a pop. It was a real tulip—that was plain enough now—but, sitting on the green pistil in the middle of the flower, was a tiny little girl. She was delicately pretty and no taller than your thumb, so she was given the name of Thumbelina.

A nicely varnished walnut-shell did for her cradle, blue violet petals for her mattress, and a rose-leaf for her counterpane. That was where she slept at night; but in the daytime she played about on the table, where the woman had put a plate with a wreath of flowers. These dipped their stalks down into the water, in the middle of which floated a large tulip petal where Thumbelina could sit and row herself from one side of the plate to the other, using a couple of white horsehairs as oars. It was a most charming sight. She could sing, too, in the sweetest little voice you ever heard.

One night, as she lay in her pretty bed, a hideous toad came hopping in through a broken pane in the window. It was a great ugly slimy toad, and it jumped straight down on to the table where Thumbelina was lying asleep under her red rose-leaf.

"She would make a nice wife for my son", thought the toad, and she snatched up the walnut-shell in which Thumbelina was sleeping and hopped off with her through the window into the garden.

There was a wide brook running through it, but the bank was swampy and muddy, and here the toad lived with her son. Ugh! wasn't he ugly and horrible—just like his mother! "Koax, koax, brekke-ke-kex!" was all he could say, when he saw the pretty little girl in the walnut-shell.

" 'Sh! Not so loud, or you'll wake her," said the old toad. "She might yet run away from us, for she's as light as swan's-down. Let's put her out in the brook on one of those broad water-lilies. She's so small and light that its leaf will be like an island for her. She can't escape from there, and in the meantime we'll get the best room ready under the mud for you two to live in."

There were quite a lot of water-lilies growing on the water with their broad green leaves which seem to be floating on the surface. The biggest of them all happened to be the furthest away, but the old toad swam out and placed the walnut-shell on it with Thumbelina still sleeping inside.

Early the next morning the poor little thing woke up and, when she saw where she was, she began to cry bitterly, for the big green leaf had water all round it and she couldn't possibly reach the bank.

The old toad stayed down in the mud and decorated her room with rushes and yellow water-lilies, so as to make everything quite snug for her new daughter-in-law. Then she swam out with her son to the water-lily where Thumbelina was standing, for they wanted to fetch that fine walnut bed and put it up in the bridal-chamber before she came herself. The old toad made a low curtsey to her in the water and said, "Here's my son—he's to be your husband. You'll have a lovely home together down in the mud."

"Koax, koax, brekke-ke-kex!" was all that the son could say.

Then they took the pretty little bed and swam away with it. But Thumbelina sat all alone on the green leaf and cried, for she didn't want to live with the horrible toad or to marry her ugly son. The little fishes, swimming down there in the water, had caught sight of the toad and heard what she said. So they poked their heads out of the water; they were so anxious to have a look at the little girl. Directly they saw her, they found her charming, and they couldn't bear to think that she must go and live with the ugly toad. No, that must never happen! They all swarmed together down in the water round the green stalk that held the leaf she was standing on and gnawed it through with their teeth; whereupon the leaf floated away with Thumbelina down the brook, far away where the toad could never reach her.

Thumbelina went sailing past all sorts of places, and the little birds perched in the bushes saw her and trilled out, "What a pretty little lady!" The leaf that carried her floated further and further on; and thus it was that Thumbelina began her journey abroad.

A dainty little white butterfly kept on fluttering round and round her, till at last it settled on the leaf, for it had taken a great liking for Thumbelina; and she too was pleased, because the toad couldn't reach her now and she was sailing through such a lovely part of the brook. The sunshine gleamed on the water like the finest gold. Then she took her sash and tied one end of it round the butterfly, while the other end she made fast to the leaf; and this at once gathered speed—and so did Thumbelina because, you see, she was standing on the leaf. Just then a large cockchafer came flying up and, catching sight of her, clutched her round her slender waist and flew with

her up into a tree. But the green leaf went floating on and the butterfly with it, because it had been tied to the leaf and couldn't manage to free itself.

Gracious, what a fright it gave poor Thumbelina, when the cockchafer flew up into the tree with her! Still, what upset her even more was the thought of the pretty white butterfly that she had tied to the leaf; for, unless it could manage to free itself, it would certainly starve to death. But that didn't worry the cockchafer in the slightest. He settled beside her on the largest green leaf in the tree, gave her some nectar from the blossoms and said how pretty she was, although she wasn't a bit like a cockchafer. Later on, all the other cockchafers living in the tree came to call on her. They stared at Thumbelina, and the young lady cockchafers shrugged their feelers—"Why, she's only got two legs", they said. "What a pitiable sight!" "She hasn't any feelers", they went on. "She's so pinched in at the waist—ugh! she might almost be a human. Isn't she ugly!" exclaimed all the lady cockchafers.

And yet Thumbelina was really so pretty. And that's what the cockchafer thought who had carried her off; but when all the others kept saying how ugly she was, then at length he thought so too and would have nothing to do with her; she could go where she liked. They flew with her down from the tree and sat her on a daisy. There she cried and cried, because she was so ugly that the cock-chafers wouldn't have her; and all the time she was as beautiful as can be—as exquisite as the loveliest rose-petal.

Right through the summer poor Thumbelina lived quite alone in that enormous wood. She took blades of grass and plaited herself a bed, which she hung under a large dockleaf, so as to be out of the rain. She got her food from the honey in the flowers, and her drink from the morning dew on the leaves; and in this way summer and autumn went by. But now came winter—the long, cold winter. All the birds that had sung to her so beautifully now flew away; the trees and flowers withered; the great dock-leaf she had been living under furled itself into nothing but a faded yellow stalk. She felt the cold most terribly, for her clothes were by this time in tatters, and she herself was so tiny and delicate, poor Thumbelina, that she would surely be frozen to death. It began snowing, and every snowflake that fell on her was like a whole shovelful being thrown on us, for we are quite big and she was no taller than your thumb. So she wrapped herself up in a dead leaf, but there was no warmth in that, and she shivered with cold.

On the fringe of the wood where she had now come to was a large cornfield; but the corn had long been harvested, and only the bare barren stubble thrust up from the frozen earth. It was just like an entire forest for her to walk through—oh, and she was shivering with cold! At length she came to the field-mouse's door. It was a little hole down below the stubble. There the field-mouse had a fine snug place to live in, with a whole roomful of corn and a splendid kitchen and dining-room. Poor Thumbelina stood just inside the door like any other wretched beggar-girl and asked for a little bit of barley-corn, for she hadn't had a scrap to eat for two days.

"You poor mite!" said the field-mouse, for at heart she was a kind old thing. "Come you in and have a bite with me in my warm room."

As she at once took a liking to Thumbelina she made a suggestion. "You're quite welcome to stay with me for the winter," she said, "as long as you'll keep my rooms nice and tidy and also tell me stories, for I'm so fond of stories." And Thumbelina did what the kind old field-mouse asked for and was extremely comfortable there.

"I dare say we shall have a visitor before long", said the field-mouse. "My neighbour generally pays me a call once a week. His house is even snugger than mine, with good-sized rooms, and he wears such a lovely black velvet coat. If only you could get him for a husband, you'd be comfortably off. But his sight's very bad. You must tell him all the nicest stories you know".

Thumbelina took no notice of all this; she

107

had no intention of marrying the neighbour, for he was a mole. He came and called in his black velvet coat. He was so rich and clever, according to the field-mouse, and his home was twenty times the size of the field-mouse's. He was very learned, but he couldn't bear sunshine and pretty flowers; he said all sorts of nasty things about them, never having seen them. Thumbelina had to sing, and she sang both "Ladybird, ladybird, fly away home" and "Ring-a-ring-o'roses"; and the mole fell in love with her because of her pretty voice, but he didn't say anything— he was much too cautious a man for that.

He had lately dug a long passage for himself through the earth, leading from his house to theirs. Here the field-mouse and Thumbelina were invited to stroll whenever they cared to. But he told them not to be afraid of the dead bird lying in the passage; it was a whole bird with beak and feathers, that had evidently only just died as the winter began and was now buried in the very spot where he had made his underground passage.

The mole took a bit of touchwood in his mouth—for in the dark that shines just like fire—and went ahead to give them a light in the long dark passage. When they came to where the dead bird was lying, the mole tilted his broad snout up to the ceiling and thrust through the earth; making a large hole through which the light could penetrate. In the middle of the floor lay a dead swallow with its pretty wings folded close in to its sides, and head and legs tucked in beneath its feathers. The poor bird must have died of cold. Thumbelina felt so sorry for it; she was very fond of all the little birds that had sung and twittered for her so sweetly right through the summer. But the mole kicked at it with his stumpy legs, saying, "That won't chirp any more! How wretched it must be to be born a little bird! Thank goodness no child of mine ever will be. A bird like that has of course nothing but its twitter and is bound to starve to death when winter comes."

"Just what I'd expect to hear from a sensible man like you", said the field-mouse.

109

"What has a bird to show for all its twittering, when winter comes? It must starve and freeze. But I suppose that's considered a great thing."

Thumbelina didn't say a word, but when the other two turned their backs on the bird, she stooped down and, smoothing aside the feathers that lay over its head, she kissed its closed eyes. "Who knows—this may be the very one", she thought, "that used to sing so beautifully to me last summer."

The mole now filled in the hole where the daylight shone through and saw the two ladies home. But that night Thumbelina simply couldn't sleep; so she got up and plaited a fine big blanket of hay, which she carried down and spread all over the dead bird, and she took some soft cotton-wool she had found in the field-mouse's room and tucked this in at the sides, so that the bird might lie warm in the cold earth.

"Goodbye, you lovely little bird," she said. "Goodbye, and thank you for your beautiful singing last summer, when all the trees were green and the sun was so bright and warm". Then she laid her head up against the bird's breast—but at the same moment she got such a fright, for she heard a kind of thumping inside. It was the bird's heart. The bird wasn't dead; it had been lying numb and unconscious and now, as it grew warm again, it revived.

You see, in autumn the swallows all fly away to the warm countries, but if there's one that lags behind it gets so cold that it falls down dead. There it lies, where it fell, and the cold snow covers it over.

Thumbelina was all of a tremble from the fright she had, for the bird was of course an immense great creature beside her, who was no taller than your thumb. However, she took courage and tucked the cotton-wool still more closely round the poor swallow and fetched a curled mint leaf that she had been using herself for a counterpane and spread this over the bird's head.

The following night she again stole down to the bird, and this time it had quite revived; but it was so feeble that it could only open its eyes for a short moment to look at

Thumbelina, standing there with a bit of touchwood in her hand, for she had no other light.

"Thank you, my darling child," said the sick swallow. "I'm lovely and warm now. I shall soon get back my strength and be able to fly again, out in the warm sunshine."

"Ah, but it's so cold out of doors", she said. "It's snowing and freezing. Stay in your warm bed; I'll look after you all right."

Then she brought the swallow some water, in the petal of a flower, and the bird drank it and told her how it had torn one of its wings on a bramble and therefore couldn't fly as fast as the other swallows when they flew far, far away to the warm countries. At last it had fallen to the ground, but it couldn't remember anything after that and had no idea how it came to be where it was.

The swallow now remained here all through the winter, and Thumbelina took care of it and grew very fond of it. Neither the mole nor the field-mouse heard anything at all about this; they had no liking for the poor wretched swallow.

As soon as spring had arrived and the sun had begun to warm the earth, the swallow said goodbye to Thumbelina, who opened up the hole that the mole had made in the roof of the passage. The sun came shining in so pleasantly, and the swallow asked if she would like to come too; she could sit on its back, and they would fly far out into the green forest. But Thumbelina knew that it would grieve the old field-mouse, if she left her like that.

"No, I can't", said Thumbelina. "Goodbye, goodbye, you dear kind girl", said the swallow, as it flew into the open sunshine. Thumbelina gazed after it with tears in her eyes, for she was so fond of the poor swallow.

"Tweet-tweet!" sang the bird and flew off into the woods ...

Thumbelina felt so sad. She was never allowed to go out into the warm sunshine. The corn that had been sown in the field above the field-mouse's home was certainly very tall; so that it was like a dense wood for the poor little girl, who after all was only an inch high.

"You will have to start making your wedding trousseau this summer," the field-mouse told her, because by now their neighbour, the tiresome tedious mole in the black velvet coat, had proposed to her. "You'll need to have both woollens and linen—something for every occasion—when you're married to the mole."

So Thumbelina had to spin from a distaff, and the field-mouse engaged four spiders to spin and weave day and night. Every evening there was a visit from the mole, who always kept on about how, when summer was over, the sun wasn't nearly so warm, whereas now it scorched the earth till it was as hard as a stone. Yes, and when the summer had ended there was to be his wedding with Thumbelina. But she wasn't at all pleased, for she found the mole such a terrible bore. Every morning, as the sun rose, and every evening as it set, she stole out to the door, and when the wind parted the ears of corn so that she could see the blue sky, she thought how lovely and bright it was out there and did so wish she could

114

catch sight of the dear swallow once more; but the bird never came again and had evidently flown far off into the beautiful green forest.

Now it was autumn, and Thumbelina had the whole of her trousseau ready.

"Your wedding will be in four weeks' time", the field-mouse told her. But Thumbelina wept and said she wouldn't marry the tedious mole.

"Hoity-toity!" said the field-mouse. "Don't you be so pig-headed, or I'll bite you with my white teeth. Why, he's a splendid husband for you. The Queen herself hasn't anything like his black velvet coat. His kitchen and cellar are both of the best. You ought to thank Heaven he's yours."

The wedding-day arrived. The mole was already there to fetch Thumbelina. She would have to live with him deep down under the earth and never come out into the warm sunshine, for he didn't care for that. The poor child was very sad at having to say goodbye to the beautiful sun, which she had at least been allowed to look at from the doorway when she was living with the field-mouse.

"Goodbye, bright sun!" she said and, stretching out her arms to it, she also took a few steps out from the field-mouse's dwelling; for the harvest was in, and nothing was left but the dry stubble. "Goodbye, goodbye", she said, throwing her tiny arms round a little red flower standing near. "Remember me to the dear swallow, if you happen to see it."

"Tweet-tweet!" she heard suddenly over her head. She looked up, and there was the swallow just passing. How delighted it was to see Thumbelina! She told the bird how she disliked having to marry the ugly mole and to live deep down under the earth where the sun never shone. She couldn't help crying at the thought.

"The cold winter will soon be here", said the swallow. "I'm going far away to the warm countries. Will you come with me? You can sit on my back. Just tie yourself on with your sash, and away we'll fly from the ugly mole and his dingy house, far away across the mountains, to the warm countries, where the sun shines more brightly than it does here and there's always summer with its lovely flowers. Dear little Thumbelina, do come with me—you who saved my life when I lay frozen stiff in that dismal cellar."

"Yes, I'll come with you", said Thumbelina. She climbed on to the bird's back, setting her feet on its outstretched wings and tieing her sash to one of the strongest feathers. Then the swallow flew high up into the air, over lake and forest, high up over the great mountains of eternal snow. Thumbelina shivered in the cold air, but then she snuggled in under the bird's warm feathers, merely poking out her little head to look at all the loveliness stretched out beneath her.

And at last they reached the warm countries. The sun was shining there much more brightly than with us, and the sky looked twice as far off. On walls and slopes grew the finest black and white grapes, in the woods hung lemons and oranges; the air smelt sweetly of myrtle and curled mint, and the most delightful children darted about on

the roads playing with large gay-coloured
butterflies. But the swallow kept flying on
and on, and the country became more and
more beautiful, till at last they came upon
an ancient palace of glittering white marble
standing among vivid green trees beside a
blue lake. Vines went curling up round the
tall pillars, and right at the top were a number of swallow's nests. One of these was the
home of the swallow that had brought
Thumbelina on its back.

"Here's my house", cried the swallow.
"But you see those beautiful flowers growing
down there? You shall now choose one of
them yourself, and then I'll put you on it,
and you can make yourself as cosy as you
like.

"That will be lovely", she said, clapping
her little hands.

A large white marble column was lying
there on the ground just as it had fallen and
broken into three pieces, but in among these
were growing the most beautiful white flowers. The swallow flew down with Thumbelina and placed her on one of the broad

118

petals — but what a surprise she got! There in the middle of the flower sat a little man as white and transparent as if he had been made of glass. He wore the neatest little gold crown on his head and the most exquisite wings on his shoulders; he himself was no bigger than Thumbelina. He was the guardian spirit of the flower. Each flower had just such a little man or woman living in it, but this one was King of them all.

"Goodness, how handsome he is!" whispered Thumbelina to the swallow. The little monarch was very frightened of the swallow, which of course seemed a gigantic bird beside one so small and delicate as himself; but when he caught sight of Thumbelina he was enchanted, for she was much the prettiest little lady he had ever seen. So he took the gold crown off his head and placed it on hers. At the same time he asked her what her name was and whether she would be his wife; if so, she would become Queen of all the flowers. Well, he would be a proper husband for her, quite different from the son of the old toad and from the mole with the black velvet coat. So she said yes to the handsome King, and from every flower there appeared a lady or a gentleman that was the most dapper little creature imaginable. Each one brought a present for Thumbelina, but the best of them all was a pair of beautiful wings from a large white fly. These were fastened to her back, so that she too could flit from flower to flower. There was such rejoicing, and the swallow sat up above in its nest and sang for them as well as it could, but the poor bird was really too sad at heart, for it was very fond of Thumbelina and would have liked never to be parted from her.

"You shan't be called Thumbelina", said the guardian spirit of the flower to her. "It's an ugly name, and you are so pretty. We will call you Maia."

"Goodbye, goodbye", said the swallow and flew away again from the warm countries, far away back to Denmark. There it had a little nest above the window where the man lives who can tell fairy tales, and there it was that the swallow sang "tweet-tweet!" to him ... And that's where the whole story comes from.

THE LITTLE MERMAID

Far out at sea the water's as blue as the petals of the loveliest cornflower, and as clear as the purest glass; but it's very deep, deeper than any anchor can reach. Many church steeples would have to be piled up one above the other to reach from the bottom of the sea to the surface. Right down there live the sea people.

Now you mustn't for a moment suppose that it's a bare white sandy bottom. Oh, no. The most wonderful trees and plants are growing down there, with stalks and leaves that bend so easily that they stir at the very slightest movement of the water, just as though they were alive. All the fishes, big ones and little ones, slip in and out of the branches just like birds in the air up here. Down in the deepest part of all is the sea King's palace. Its walls are made of coral, and the long pointed windows of the clearest amber; but the roof is made of cockleshells that open and shut with the current. It's a pretty sight, for in each shell is a dazzling pearl; any single one of them would be a splendid ornament in a Queen's crown.

The sea King down there had been a widower for some years, but his old mother kept house for him. She was a clever woman, but proud of her noble birth; that's why she went about with twelve oysters on her tail, while the rest of the nobility had to put up with only six. But apart from that, she was deserving of special praise, because she was so fond of the little sea Princesses, her grandchildren. They were six pretty children, but the youngest was the loveliest of them all. Her skin was as clear and delicate as a rose-leaf, her eyes were as blue as the deepest lake, but like the others she had no feet; her body ended in a fish's tail.

All the long day they could play down there in the palace, in the great halls where living flowers grew out of the walls. The fishes would swim in to them, just as with us the swallows fly in when we open the windows; but the fishes swam right up to the little Princesses, fed out of their hands, and let themselves be patted.

Outside the palace was a large garden with trees of deep blue and fiery red; the fruit all shone like gold, and the flowers like a blazing fire with stalks and leaves that were never still. The soil itself was the finest sand, but blue like a sulphur flame. Over everything down there lay a strange blue gleam; you really might have thought you were standing high up in the air with nothing to see but sky above and below you, rather than that you were at the bottom of the sea. When there was a dead calm you caught a glimpse of the sun, which looked like a purple flower pouring out all light from its cup.

Each of the small Princesses had her own

little plot in the garden, where she could dig and plant at will. One of them gave her flower-bed the shape of a whale, another thought it nicer for hers to look like a little mermaid; but the youngest made hers quite round like the sun, and would only have flowers that shone red like it. She was a curious child, silent and thoughtful; and when the other sisters decorated their gardens with the most wonderful things they had got from sunken ships, she would have nothing but the rose-red flowers that were like the sun high above, and a beautiful marble statue. It was the statue of a handsome boy, hewn from the clear white stone and come down to the bottom of the sea from a wreck. Beside the statue she planted a rose-red weeping willow, which grew splendidly and let its fresh foliage droop over the statue right down to the blue sandy bottom. Here the shadow took on a violet tinge and, like the branches, was never still; roots and tree-top looked as though they were playing at kissing each other.

Nothing pleased her more than to hear

about the world of humans up above the sea. The old grandmother had to tell her all she knew about ships and towns, people and animals. One thing especially surprised her with its beauty, and this was that the flowers had a smell—at the bottom of the sea they hadn't any—and also that the woods were green and the fishes you saw in among the branches could sing as clearly and prettily as possible. It was the little birds that the grandmother called fishes; otherwise, never having seen a bird, the small sea Princesses would never have understood her.

"As soon as you are fifteen," the grandmother told them, "you shall be allowed to rise to the surface, and to sit in the moonlight on the rocks and watch the great ships sailing past; you shall see woods and towns." That coming year one of the sisters was to have her fifteenth birthday, but the rest of them—well, they were each one year younger than the other; so the youngest of them had a whole five years to wait before she could rise up from the bottom and see how things are with us. But each promised to tell

the others what she had seen and found
most interesting on the first day; for their
grandmother didn't really tell them enough
—there were so many things they were longing to hear about.

None of them was so full of longing as the youngest: the very one who had most time to wait and was so silent and thoughtful. Many a night she stood at the open window and gazed up through the dark-blue water, where the fishes frisked their tails and fins. She could see the moon and the stars, though it's true their light was rather pale; and yet through the water they looked much larger than they do to us, and if ever a kind of black cloud went gliding along below them, she knew it was either a whale swimming above her or else a vessel with many passengers; these certainly never imagined that a lovely little mermaid was standing beneath and stretching up her white hands towards the keel of their ship.

By now the eldest Princess was fifteen and allowed to go up to the surface.

When she came back, she had a hundred things to tell; but the loveliest, she said, was to lie in the moonlight on a sandbank in a calm sea and there, close in to the shore, to look at the big town where the lights were twinkling like a hundred stars; to listen to the sound of music and the noise and clatter of carts and people; to see all the towers and spires on the churches and hear the bells ringing. And just because she couldn't get there, it was this above everything that she longed for.

Oh, how the youngest sister drank it all in! And, when later in the evening she stood at the open window and gazed up through the dark-blue water, she thought of the big town with all its noise and clatter, and then she seemed to catch the sound of the church-bells ringing down to her.

The following year, the second sister was allowed to go up through the water and swim wherever she liked. She came to the surface just as the sun was setting, and that was the sight she found most beautiful. The whole sky had looked like gold, she said, and the clouds—well, she just couldn't describe how beautiful they were as they sailed, all crimson and violet, over her head. And yet, much faster than they, a flock of wild swans flew like a long white veil across the water where the sun was setting. She swam off in that direction, but the sun sank, and its rosy light was swallowed up by sea and cloud.

The year after that, the third sister went up. She was the boldest of them all, and she swam up a wide river that flowed into the sea. She saw delightful green slopes with grape-vines; manors and farms peeped out among magnificent woods; she heard all the birds singing; and the sun was so hot that she often had to dive under the water to cool her burning face. In a small cove she came upon a swarm of little human children splashing about quite naked in the water. She wanted to play with them, but they ran away terrified, and a little black animal came up; it was a dog. She had never seen a dog before. It barked at her so dreadfully that she got frightened and made for the open sea. But never could she forget the magnificent woods, the green slopes and the darling children, who could swim on the water although they had no fishes' tails.

The fourth sister was not so bold. She kept far out in the wild waste of ocean, and told them that was just what was so wonderful: you could see for miles and miles around you, and the sky hung above like a big glass bell. She had seen ships, but a long way off, looking like sea-gulls. The jolly dolphins had been turning somersaults, and enormous whales had spirted up water from their nostrils, so that they seemed to be surrounded by a hundred fountains.

And now it was the turn of the fifth sister. Her birthday happened to come in winter, and so she saw things that the others hadn't seen the first time. The sea appeared quite green, and great icebergs were floating about; they looked like pearls, she said, and yet were much larger than the church-towers put up by human beings. They were to be seen in the most fantastic shapes, and they glittered like diamonds. She had sat down on one of the biggest, and all the ships gave it a wide berth as they sailed in terror past where she sat with her long hair streaming in the wind. But late in the evening the sky became overcast with clouds; it lightened and thundered, as the dark waves lifted the great blocks of ice right up, so that they flashed in the fierce red lightning. All the ships took in sail, and, amidst the general horror and alarm, she sat calmly on her floating iceberg and watched the blue lightning zigzag into the glittering sea.

The first time one of the sisters went up to the surface, she would always be delighted to see so much that was new and beautiful; but afterwards, when they were older and could go up as often as they liked, it no longer interested them; they longed to be back again, and when a month had passed they said that, after all, it was nicest down below—it was such a comfort to be home.

Often of an evening the five sisters used to link arms and float up together out of the water. They had lovely voices, more beautiful than any human voice; and when a gale sprang up threatening shipwreck, they would swim in front of the ships and sing tempting songs of how delightful it was at the bottom of the sea. And they told the sailors not to be afraid of coming down there, but the sailors couldn't make out the words of their song; they thought it was the noise of the gale, nor did they ever see any of the delights the mermaids promised, because when the ship sank the crew were drowned, and only as dead men did they come to the palace of the sea King.

When of an evening the sisters floated up through the sea like this, arm in arm, their little sister stayed back all alone gazing after them. She would have cried, only a mermaid hasn't any tears, and so she suffers all the more.

"Oh, if only I were fifteen!" she said. "I'm sure I shall love that world up there and the people who live in it."

And then at last she was fifteen.

"There, now you'll soon be off our hands." said her grandmother, the old Dowager Queen. "Come now, let me dress you up like your sisters;" and she put a wreath of white lilies on her hair, but every petal of the flower was half a pearl. And the old lady made eight big oysters nip tight on to the Princess's tail to show her high rank.

"Oo! that hurts," said the little mermaid.

"Yes," said the grandmother, "one can't have beauty for nothing."

How she would have liked to shake off all this finery and put away the heavy wreath! The red flowers in her garden suited her much better, but she didn't dare make any change, "Goodbye," she said, and went up through the water as light and clear as a bubble.

The sun had just set, as she put her head up out of the sea, but the clouds had still a gleam of rose and gold; and up in the pale pink sky the evening star shone clear and beautiful. The air was soft and fresh, and the sea dead calm. A large three-masted ship was lying there, with only one sail hoisted because not a breath of wind was stirring, and sailors were lolling about in the rigging and on the yards. There was music and singing, and as it grew dark hundreds of lanterns were lit that, with their many different colours, looked as if the flags of all nations were flying in the breeze.

The little mermaid swam right up to the

porthole of the cabin and, every time she rose with swell of the wave, she could see through the clear glass a crowd of splendidly dressed people; but the handsomest of them all was a young Prince with large dark eyes. He couldn't have been much more than sixteen; it was his birthday, and that's why there was all this set-out. As the young Prince came out on to the deck where sailors were dancing, over a hundred rockets swished up into the sky—and broke into a glitter like broad daylight. That frightened the little mermaid, and she dived down under the water; but she quickly popped up her head again, and look! it was just as if all the stars in heaven were falling down on her. Never had she seen such fireworks. Great suns went spinning around, gorgeous fire-fishes swerving into the blue air, and all this glitter was mirrored in the clear still water. On board the ship herself it was so light that you could make out every little rope, let alone the passengers. Oh, how handsome the young Prince was; he shook hands with the sailors, he laughed and smiled, while the music went floating out into the loveliness of the night.

It grew late, but the little mermaid couldn't take her eyes off the ship and the beautiful Prince. The coloured lanterns were put out, the rockets no longer climbed into the sky, and the cannon were heard no more; but deep down in the sea there was a mumbling and a rumbling. Meanwhile the mermaid stayed on the water, rocking up and down so that she could look into the cabin. But the ship now gathered speed; one after another her sails were spread. The waves increased, heavy clouds blew up, and lightning flashed in the distance. Yes, they were in for a terrible storm; so the sailors took in their sails, as the great ship rocked and scudded through the raging sea. The waves rose higher and higher like huge black mountains, threatening to bring down the mast, but the ship dived like a swan into the trough of the waves and then rode up again on their towering crests. The little mermaid thought, why, it must be fun for a ship to sail like that—but the crew didn't. The vessel creaked and cracked, the stout planks crumpled up under the heavy pounding of the sea against the ship, the mast snapped in the middle like a stick, and then the ship gave a lurch to one side as the water came rushing into the hold. At last the little mermaid realised that they were in danger; she herself had to look out for the beams and bits of wreckage that were drifting on the water. One moment it was so pitch dark that she couldn't see a thing, but then when the lightning came it was so bright that she could make out everyone on board. It was now a case of each man for himself. The young Prince was the one she was looking for and, as the ship broke up, she saw him disappear into the depths of the sea. Just for one moment she felt quite pleased, for now he would come down to her; but then she remembered that humans can't live under the water and that only as a dead man could he come down to her father's palace. No, no, he mustn't die. So she she swam in among the drifting beams and planks, with no thought for the danger of being crushed by them; she dived deep down and came right up again among the waves, and at last she found the young Prince. He could hardly swim any longer in the heavy sea; his arms and legs were beginning to tire, the fine eyes were closed, he would certainly have drowned if the little mermaid had not come. She held his head above water and then let the waves carry her along with him wherever they pleased.

By morning the gale had quite gone; not the smallest trace of the ship was to be seen. The sun rose red and glowing out of the water and seemed to bring life to the Prince's cheeks, but his eyes were still shut. The mermaid kissed his fine high forehead and smoothed back his dripping hair. He was like the marble statue down in her little garden; she kissed him again and wished that he might live.

Presently she saw the mainland in front of her, high blue mountains with the white snow glittering on their peaks like nestling swans. Down by the shore were lovely green woods and, in front of them, a church or a convent —she wasn't sure which, but anyhow a building. Lemon and orange trees were growing in the garden, and tall palm trees in front of the gate. At this point the sea formed a little inlet, where the water was quite smooth but very deep close in to the rock where the fine white sand had silted up. She swam here with the handsome Prince and laid him on the sand with his head carefully pillowed in the warm sunshine.

Now there was a sound of bells from the large white building, and a number of young girls came through the garden. So the little mermaid swam further out behind some large boulders that were sticking out of the water and covered her hair and breast with seafoam, so that her face wouldn't show; and then she watched to see who would come to the help of the unfortunate Prince.

It wasn't long before a young girl came along. She seemed quite frightened, but only for a moment; then she fetched several others, and the mermaid saw the Prince come round and smile at those about him; but no smile came out to her, for of course he didn't know she had rescued him. She felt so sad that, when he was taken away into the large building, she dived down sorrowfully into the sea and went back to her father's palace.

Silent and thoughtful as she had always been, she now became much more so. Her sisters asked her what she had seen on her first visit to the surface, but she wouldn't say.

Many a morning and many an evening she rose up to where she had left the Prince. She saw the fruit in the garden ripen and be gathered, she saw the snow melt on the peaks, but she never saw the Prince, and so she always turned back more despondent than ever. Her one comfort was to sit in the little garden with her arms round the beautiful marble statue which was so like the Prince. She never looked after her flowers, and they grew into a sort of wilderness, out over the paths, and braided their long stalks and leaves on to the branches of the trees, until the light was quite shut out.

At last she could keep it to herself no longer, but told one of her sisters; and immediately all the rest got to know, but nobody else—except a few other mermaids who didn't breathe a word to any but their nearest friends. One of these was able to say who the Prince was; she, too, had seen the party that was held on board the ship, and knew where he came from and whereabouts his kingdom was.

"Come on, little sister!" said the other Princesses. And with arms round each other's shoulders they rose in one line out of the sea, just in front of where the Prince's castle stood. It was built in a glistening stone of pale yellow with great flights of marble steps; one of these led straight into the sea. Splendid gilt domes curved above the roof, and between the pillars that went right round the building were lifelike sculptures in marble. Through the clear glass in the tall windows you could see into the most magnificent rooms; these were hung with sumptuous silk curtains and tapestries and their walls were covered with large paintings that were a delight to the eye. In the middle of the biggest room was a huge splashing fountain; its spray was flung high up to the glass dome in the ceiling, through which the sun shone down on to the water and the beautiful plants growing in the great pool.

Now she knew where he lived, and many an evening and many a night she would come to the surface at that spot. She swam much closer to the shore than any of the others had ever dared. She even went up the narrow creek under the fine marble balcony that threw its long shadow across the water. Here she would sit and gaze at the young Prince, who imagined he was quite alone in the clear moonlight.

Often in the evening she saw him go out to the strains of music in his splendid vessel that was dressed with flags. She peeped out from among the green rushes and, when the wind caught her long silvery veil and someone saw it, they fancied it was a swan spreading its wings.

On many nights, when the fishermen were at sea with their torches, she heard them speaking so well of the young Prince, and that made her glad she had saved his life when he drifted about half-dead on the waves;

and she thought of how closely his head had rested on her bosom and how lovingly she had kissed him. But he knew nothing whatsoever about that, never even dreamed she existed.

Fonder and fonder she became of human beings, more and more she longed for their company. Their world seemed to her to be so much larger than her own. You see, they could fly across the ocean in ships, climb the tall mountains high above the clouds; and the lands they owned stretched with woods and meadows further than her eyes could see. There was so much she would have liked to know, but her sisters couldn't answer all her questions, and so she asked the old grandmother, for she knew all about the upper world—as she so aptly called the countries above the sea.

"If people don't drown," asked the little mermaid, "can they go on living for ever? Don't they die, as we do down here in the sea?"

"Yes, yes," said the old lady, "they, too, have to die; their lifetime is even shorter

143

than ours. We can live for three hundred years, but when our life here comes to an end we merely turn into foam on the water; we haven't even a grave down here among those we love. We've no immortal soul; we shall never have another life. We're like the green rush—once it's been cut it can't grow green again. But human beings have a soul which lives for ever; still lives after the body is turned to dust. The soul goes climbing up through the clear air, up till it reaches the shining stars. Just as we rise up out of the sea and look at the countries of human beings, so they rise up to beautiful unknown regions—ones we shall never see."

"Why haven't we got an immortal soul?" the little mermaid asked sadly. "I would give the whole three hundred years I have to live, to become for one day a human being and then share in that heavenly world."

"You mustn't go worrying about that," said the grandmother. "We're much happier and better off here than the people who live up there.

"So then I'm doomed to die and float like

foam on the sea, never to hear the music of the waves or see the lovely flowers and the red sun. Isn't there anything at all I can do to win an immortal soul?"

"No," said the old lady. "Only if a human being loved you so much that you were more to him than father and mother—if he clung to you with all his heart and soul, and let the priest put his right hand in yours as a promise to be faithful and true here and in all eternity—then his soul would flow over into your body and you, too, would get a share in human happiness. He would give you a soul and yet keep his own. But that can never happen. The very thing that's so beautiful here in the sea, your fish's tail, seems ugly to people on the earth; they know so little about it that they have to have two clumsy supports called legs, in order to look nice."

That made the little mermaid sigh and look sadly at her fish's tail.

"We must be content," said the old lady. "Let's dance and be gay for the three hundred years we have to live—that's a good time, isn't it?—then one can have one's fill of sleep in the grave all the more pleasantly afterwards. To-night we're having a Court ball."

That was something more magnificent than we ever see on the earth. In the great ball-room walls and ceiling were made of thick but quite clear glass. Several hundred enormous shells, rose-red and grass-green, were ranged on either side, each with a blue-burning flame which lit up the whole room and, shining out through the walls, lit up the sea outside as well. Countless fishes, big and small, could be seen swimming towards the glass walls; the scales on some of them shone purple-red, and on others like silver and gold . . . Through the middle of the ballroom flowed a wide running stream, on which mermen and mermaids danced to their own beautiful singing. No human beings have voices so lovely. The little mermaid sang the most sweetly of them all, and they clapped their hands for her, and for a moment there was joy in her heart, for she knew that she had the most beautiful voice on earth or sea.

But then her thoughts soon returned to the world above her; she couldn't forget the handsome Prince and her sorrow at not possessing, like him, an immortal soul. So she crept out of her father's palace and, while all in there was song and merriment, she sat grieving in her little garden. Suddenly she caught the sound of a horn echoing down through the water, and she thought, "Ah, there he is, sailing up above —he whom I love more than father or mother, he who is always in my thoughts and in whose hands I would gladly place the happiness of my life. I will dare anything to win him and an immortal soul. While my sisters are dancing there in my father's palace, I will go to the sea witch; I've always been dreadfully afraid of her, but perhaps she can help me and tell me what to do."

So the little mermaid left her garden and set off for the place where the witch lived, on the far side of the roaring whirlpools. She had never been that way before. There were no flowers growing, no sea grass, nothing but the bare grey sandy bottom stretching right up to the whirlpools, where the water went swirling round like roaring mill-wheels and pulled everything it could clutch down with it to the depths. She had to pass through the middle of these battering eddies in order to get to the sea witch's domain; and here, for a long stretch, there was no other way than over hot bubbling mud —the witch called it her swamp. Her house lay behind it in the middle of an extraordinary wood. All the trees and bushes were polyps, half animals and half plants. They looked like hundred-headed snakes growing out of the earth; all the branches were long slimy arms with supple worm-like fingers, and joint by joint from the root up to the very tip they were continuously on the move. They wound themselves tight round everything they could clutch hold of in the sea, and they never let go. The little mermaid was terribly scared as she paused at the edge of the wood. Her heart was throbbing with fear; she nearly turned back. But then she remembered the Prince and the human soul, and that gave her courage. She wound her

long flowing hair tightly round her head, so
that the polyps shouldn't have that to clutch
her by, she folded both her hands across her
breast and darted off just as a fish darts
through the water, in among the hideous
polyps which reached out for her with their
supple arms and fingers. She noticed how
each of them had something they had caught,
held fast by a hundred little arms like
hoops of iron. White skeletons of folk who
had been lost at sea and had sunk to the
bottom looked out from the arms of the
polyps. Ship's rudders and chests were grip-
ped tight, skeletons of land animals, and—
most horrible of all—a small mermaid whom
they had caught and throttled.

Now she came to a large slimy open space
in the wood where big fat water-snakes were
frisking about and showing their hideous
whitish-yellow bellies. In the middle was a
house built of the bones of human folk who
had been wrecked. There sat the sea witch,
letting a toad feed out of her mouth, just as
we might let a little canary come and peck
sugar. She called the horrible fat water-snakes

149

her little chicks and allowed them to sprawl about her great spongy bosom.

"I know well enough what you're after," said the sea witch. "How stupid of you! Still, you shall have your way, and it'll bring you into misfortune, my lovely Princess. You want to get rid of your fish's tail and in its place have a couple of stumps to walk on like a human being, so that the young Prince can fall in love with you and you can win him and an immortal soul"—and with that the witch gave such a loud repulsive laugh that the toad and the snakes fell to the ground and remained sprawling there. "You've just come at the right time," said the witch. "Tomorrow, once the sun's up, I could't help you for another year. I shall make you a drink, and before sunrise you must swim to land, sit down on the shore and drink it up. Then your tail will divide in two and shrink into what humans call 'pretty legs'. But it'll hurt; it'll be like a sharp sword going through you. Everyone who sees you will say you are the loveliest human child they have ever seen. You will keep your graceful move-

ments—no dancer can glide so lightly— but every step you take will feel as if you were treading on a sharp knife, enough to make your feet bleed. Are you ready to bear all that? If you are. I'll help you."

"Yes," said the little mermaid, and her voice trembled; but she thought of her Prince and the prize of an immortal soul.

"Still, don't forget this," said the witch: "once you've got human shape, you can never become a mermaid again. You can never go down through the water to your sisters and to your father's palace; and if you don't win the Prince's love, so that he forgets father and mother for you and always has you in his thoughts and lets the priest join your hands together to be man and wife, then you won't get an immortal soul. The first morning after the Prince marries someone else, your heart must break and you become foam on the water."

"I'm ready," said the little mermaid, pale as death.

"Then there's me to be paid," said the witch, "and you're not getting my help for nothing. You have the loveliest voice of all down here at the bottom of the sea. With that voice, no doubt, you think to enchant him; but that voice you shall hand over to me. I demand the best that you have for me to make a rich drink. You see, I have to give you my own blood, in order that the drink may be as sharp as a two-edged sword."

"But if you take my voice," said the little mermaid, "what shall I have left?"

"Your lovely form," said the witch, "your graceful movements, and your speaking eyes. With those you can so easily enchant a human heart ... Well, where's your spunk? Put out your little tongue and let me cut it off in payment; then you shall be given the potent mixture."

"Go on, then," said the little mermaid, and the witch put the kettle on for brewing the magic drink. "Cleanliness before everything," she said, as she scoured out the kettle with a bundle of snakes she had knotted together. Next, she scratched her breast and let her black blood drip down into the kettle; the steam took on the weirdest shapes, terrifying to look at. The witch kept popping fresh things into the kettle, and when it boiled up properly it sounded like a crocodile in tears. At last the brew was ready; it looked like the clearest water.

"There you are!" said the witch and cut off the little mermaid's tongue; she was now dumb and could neither sing nor speak.

"If the polyps should catch hold of you, as you go back through the wood," said the witch, "throw but a single drop of this drink on them, and their arms and fingers will burst into a thousand pieces." But the little mermaid had no need to do that. The polyps shrank from her in terror when they saw the dazzling drink that shone in her hand like a glittering star. So she quickly came through the wood, the swamp and the roaring whirlpools.

She could see her father's palace; the lights were out in the great ballroom. They were all certain to be asleep in there by this time; but she didn't anyhow dare to look for them, now that she was dumb and was going to leave them for ever. She felt as if her heart

154

must break for grief. She stole into the garden, picked one flower from each of her sisters' flower-beds, blew a thousand finger kisses towards the palace, and rose then through the dark-blue sea.

The sun was not yet up, as she sighted the Prince's castle and climbed the magnificent marble steps. The moon was shining wonderfully clear. The little mermaid drank the sharp burning potion, and it was as if a two-edged sword pierced through her delicate body—she fainted and lay as though dead. Then the sun, streaming over the sea, woke her up, and she felt a sharp pain. But there in front of her stood the handsome young Prince. He stared at her with his coal-black eyes, so that she cast down her own—and saw that her fish's tail had gone and she had the sweetest little white legs that any young girl could wish for; but she was quite naked, and so she wrapped herself in her long flowing hair. The Prince asked who she was and how she had come there, and she could only look back at him so gently and yet so sadly out of her deep-blue eyes; for of

155

course she couldn't speak. Then he took her by the hand and led her into the castle. Every step she took, as the witch had foretold, was as though she were treading on sharp knives and pricking gimlets; but she gladly put up with that. By the side of the Prince she went along as lightly as a bubble; and he and all of them marvelled at the charm of her graceful movements.

Costly dresses were given her of silk and muslin; she was the most beautiful in all the castle. But she was dumb; she could neither sing nor speak. Lovely slave-girls in gold and silk came out and danced before the Prince and his royal parents; one of them sang more beautifully than all the rest, and the Prince clapped his hands and smiled at her. This saddened the little mermaid, for she knew that she herself had sung far more beautifully. And she thought, "Oh, if only he knew that I gave my voice away for ever, in order to be with him!"

Next, the slave-girls danced a graceful gliding dance to the most delightful music; and then the little mermaid raised her pretty white arms, lingered on the tips of her toes and then glided across the floor, dancing as no one had danced before. She looked more and more lovely with every movement, and her eyes spoke more deeply to the heart than the slave-girls' singing.

Everyone was enchanted, and especially the Prince, who called her his little foundling. Still she went on dancing, although every time her foot touched the ground it felt as though she was treading on sharp knives. The Prince said that she must never leave him, and she was allowed to sleep on a velvet cushion outside his door.

He had boys' clothes made for her, so that she could go riding with him on horseback. They rode through the sweet-smelling woods, where the green boughs grazed her shoulders and the little birds sang among the cool foliage. She went climbing with the Prince up high mountains and, although her delicate feet bled so that others could see it, she only laughed and went on and on with him, until they could see the clouds sailing below them like a flock of birds migrating to other lands.

157

Back at the Prince's castle, when at night the others were asleep, she would go out on to the broad marble steps and cool her tingling feet in the cold sea-water; and then she would think of those down there in the depths of the sea.

One night her sisters rose up arm in arm, singing so mournfully as they swam on the water. She made signs to them, and they recognised her and told her how unhappy she had made them all. After that, they used to visit her every night; and once, in the far distance, she saw her old grandmother who hadn't been above the water for many years, and also the sea King wearing his crown. They both stretched out their hands towards her, but they didn't venture in so near to the shore as the five sisters.

Day by day she became dearer to the Prince. He loved her as one loves a dear good child, but he didn't dream of making her his Queen; and yet she had to become his wife, or else she would never win an immortal soul, but on his wedding morning would be turned to foam on the sea.

"Do you like me best of all?" the little mermaid's eyes seemed to say, when he took her in his arms and kissed her lovely brow.

"Yes," said the Prince, "you're the dearest of all, because you have the kindest heart. You are the most devoted to me, and you remind me of a young girl I once saw but shall probably never see again. I was sailing in a ship that was wrecked; the waves drove me ashore near a sacred temple where a number of young girls were serving. The youngest, who found me on the beach and saved my life—I only saw her twice. She was the only one I could ever love in this world, but you are so like her that you almost take the place of her image in my heart. She belongs to the holy temple, so that fortune has been kind in sending you to me. We will never part."

"Ah, little does he know that it was I who saved his life," thought the mermaid; "that I carried him across the sea to the temple in the wood; that I waited in the foam and watched if anyone would come. I saw the pretty girl he loves better than me"—and the mermaid sighed deeply, for she didn't know how to cry. "The girl belongs to the sacred temple, he says; she'll never come out into the world, and they'll never meet again. I am with him, I see him every day. I will take care of him, love him, give up my life to him."

But now the Prince was getting married, they said—married to the pretty daughter of the neighbouring King, and that was why he was fitting out such a splendid ship. The Prince was going off to take a look at his neighbour's kingdom—that was how they put it, meaning that it was really to take a look at his neighbour's daughter. A large suite was to go with him, but the little mermaid shook her head and laughed. She knew the Prince's thoughts far better than all the others. "I shall have to go," he had said to her. "I shall have to visit the pretty Princess, as my parents are so insistent. But force me to bring her back here as my wife, that they will never do. I can't love her. She's not like the beautiful girl in the temple, as you are. If I ever had to find a bride, I would

160

rather have you, my dear mute foundling with the speaking eyes," and he kissed her red mouth, played with her long hair and laid his head against her heart, so that it dreamed of human happiness and an immortal soul.

"You've no fear of the sea, have you, my dumb child?" he asked, as they stood on board the splendid ship that was to take him to the neighbouring kingdom. And he told her of stormy gales and dead calms, of strange fishes at the bottom of the ocean, and all that the diver had seen there; and she smiled at his tales, for she knew better than anyone else about the bottom of the sea.

At night, when there was an unclouded moon and all were asleep but the helmsman at his wheel, she sat by the ship's rail and stared down through the clear water; and she seemed to see her father's palace, with her old grandmother standing on the top of it in her silver crown and gazing up through the swift current at the keel of the vessel. Then her sisters came up on to the water and looked at her with eyes full of sorrow, wringing their white hands. She beckoned to them and smiled and would have liked to tell them that all was going well and happily with her; but the cabin-boy came up at that moment, and the sisters dived down, so that the boy felt satisfied that the white something he had seen was foam on the water.

Next morning the ship sailed into the harbour of the neighbouring King's magnificent capital. The church-bells all rang out; and trumpets were blown from the tall battlements, while the soldiers saluted with gleaming bayonets and flying colours. Every day there was a fête. Balls and parties were given one after another, but nothing had yet been seen of the Princess; it was said that she was being educated abroad in a sacred temple, where she had lessons in all the royal virtues. At last she arrived.

The little mermaid was eager for a glimpse of her beauty, and she had to admit that she had never seen anyone more charming to look at. Her complexion was so clear and delicate, and behind the long dark lashes smiled a pair of trusting deep-blue eyes.

"It's you!" cried the Prince. "You who rescued me, when I was lying half-dead on the shore." And he clasped his blushing bride in his arms. "Oh, I'm too, too happy," he said to the little mermaid. "My dearest wish—more than I ever dared to hope for —has been granted me. My happiness will give you pleasure, because you're fonder of me than any of the others." Then the little mermaid kissed his hand, and already she felt as if her heart was breaking. The morrow of his wedding would mean death to her and change her to foam on the sea.

All the church-bells were ringing, as the heralds rode round the streets to proclaim the betrothal. On every altar sweet oil was burning in rich lamps of silver. The priests swung their censers, and bride and bridegroom joined hands and received the blessing of the bishop. Dressed in silk and gold, the little mermaid stood holding the bride's train; but her ears never heard the festive music, her eyes never saw the holy rites; she was thinking of her last night on earth, of all she had lost in this world.

That same evening, bride and bridegroom went on board the ship; the cannon thundered, the flags were all flying, and amidships they had put up a royal tent of gold and purple, strewn with luxurious cushions; here the wedded couple were to sleep that calm cool night.

The sails filled with the breeze and the ship glided lightly and smoothly over the clear water.

As darkness fell, coloured lanterns were lit, and the crew danced merrily on the deck. The little mermaid could not help thinking of the first time she came up out of the sea and gazed on just such a scene of joy and splendour. And now she joined in the dance. swerving and swooping as lightly as a swallow that avoids pursuit; and shouts of admiration greeted her on every side. Never had she danced so brilliantly. It was as if sharp knives were wounding her delicate feet, but she never felt it; more painful was the wound in her heart. She knew that this was the last evening she would see the Prince for whom she had turned her back on kindred and home, given up her beautiful voice, and every day suffered hours of agony without his suspecting a thing. This was the last night she would breathe the same air as he, gaze on the deep sea and the star-blue sky. An endless night, without thoughts, without dreams, awaited her who had no soul and could never win one ... All was joy and merriment on board until long past midnight. She laughed and danced with the thought of death in her heart. The Prince kissed his lovely bride, and she toyed with his dark hair, and arm in arm they went to rest in the magnificent tent.

The ship was now hushed and still; only the helmsman was there at his wheel. And the little mermaid leaned with her white arms on the rail and looked eastward for a sign of the pink dawn. The first ray of the sun, she knew, would kill her. Suddenly she saw her sisters rising out of the sea. They were pale, like her; no more was their beautiful long hair fluttering in the wind—it had been cut off.

"We have given it to the witch, so that she

might help us to save you from dying when to-night is over. She has given us a knife—look, here it is—do you see how sharp it is? Before sunrise you must stab it into the Prince's heart. Then, when his warm blood splashes over your feet, they will grow together into a fish's tail, and you will become a mermaid once more; you will be able to come down to us in the water and live out your three hundred years before being changed into the dead salt foam of the sea. Make haste! Either he or you must die before the sun rises. Our old grandmother has been sorrowing till her white hair has fallen away, as ours fell before the witch's scissors. Kill the Prince and come back to us! But make haste—look at that red gleam in the sky. In a few minutes the sun will rise, and then you must die." And with a strange deep sigh they sank beneath the waves.

The little mermaid drew aside the purple curtain of the tent, and she saw the lovely bride sleeping with her head on the Prince's breast. She stooped and kissed his handsome brow, looked at the sky where the pink dawn glowed brighter and brighter, looked at the sharp knife in her hand, and again fixed her eyes on the Prince, who murmured in his dreams the name of his bride—she alone was in his thoughts. The knife quivered in the mermaid's hand—but then she flung it far out into the waves; they glimmered red where it fell, and what looked like drops of blood came oozing out of the water. With a last glance at the Prince from eyes half-dimmed in death she hurled herself from the ship into the sea and felt her body dissolving into foam.

And now the sun came rising from the sea. Its rays fell gentle and warm on the death-chilled foam, and the little mermaid had no feeling of death. She saw the bright sun and, hovering above her, hundreds of lovely creatures—she could see right through them, see the white sails of the ship and the pink clouds in the sky. And their voice was the voice of melody, yet so spiritual that no human ear could hear it, just as no earthly eye could see them. They had no wings, but their own lightness bore them up as they floated through the air. The little mermaid saw that she had a body like theirs, raising itself freer and freer from the foam.

"To whom am I coming?" she asked, and her voice sounded like that of the other beings, more spiritual than any earthly music can record.

"To the daughters of the air," answered the others. "A mermaid has no immortal soul and can never have one unless she wins the love of a mortal. Eternity, for her, depends on a power outside her. Neither have the daughters of the air an everlasting soul, but by good deeds they can shape one for themselves. We shall fly to the hot countries, where the stifling air of pestilence means death to mankind; we shall bring them cool breezes. We shall scatter the fragrance of flowers through the air and send them comfort and healing. When for three hundred years we have striven to do the good we can, then we shall win an immortal soul and have a share in mankind's eternal happiness. You, poor little mermaid, have striven for that with all your heart; you have suffered and endured, and have raised yourself into the world of the spirits of the air. Now, by three hundred years of good deeds, you too can shape for yourself an immortal soul."

And the little mermaid raised her crystal arms towards God's sun, and for the first time she knew the feeling of tears.

On board the ship there was bustle and life once more. She saw the Prince with his pretty bride looking about for her; sorrowfully they stared at the heaving foam, as if they knew she had thrown herself into the waves. Unseen, she kissed the forehead of the bride, gave a smile to the Prince, and then with the other children of the air she climbed to a rose-red cloud that was sailing in the sky.

"So we shall float for three hundred years, till at last we come into the heavenly kingdom."

"And we may reach it even sooner," whispered one. "Unseen we float into human homes where there are children and, for every day we find a good child who makes father and mother happy and earns their love, God shortens our time of trial. The child never knows when we fly through the room and, if that makes us smile with joy, then a year is taken away from the three hundred. But if we see a child who is naughty or spiteful, then we have to weep tears of sorrow, **and every tear adds one** more day to our time of trial."

THE EMPEROR'S NEW
CLOTHES

Many years ago there lived an Emperor who was so tremendously fond of fine new clothes that he spent all his money on being elegantly dressed. He took no interest in his army or the theatre or in driving through the country, unless it was to shew off his new clothes. He had different clothes for every hour of the day and, just as you might say of a King that he was in the

171

council-chamber, so it was always said of the Emperor: "He's in his wardrobe."

There was plenty of fun going on in the city where the Emperor lived. Strangers were continually arriving, and one day there came two swindlers. They made out they were weavers and could weave the very finest stuffs imaginable. Not only were colours and design unusually attractive, but the clothes made from their material had the peculiarity of being invisible to anyone who wasn't fit for his post or who was hopelessly stupid.

"I say! They must be wonderful clothes," thought the Emperor. "If I had some, I could find out which of my statesmen were unfit for their posts and also be able to tell the clever ones from the stupid. Yes, I must have some of that stuff woven for me at once." And he paid down a large sum of money to the swindlers straight away, so as to enable them to start work.

And they did; they put up a couple of looms and pretended to be working, although there was absolutely nothing in the loom. They coolly demanded the most delicate silk and the finest gold thread, which they promptly stowed away in their own bags; and then they went on working far into the night at their empty looms.

"Well, now, I wonder how they are getting on with the work," said the Emperor to himself. But there was one point that really made him feel rather anxious, namely, that a man who was stupid or quite unfit for his post would never be able to see what was woven. Not that he need have any fears for himself—he was quite confident about that —but all the same it might be better to send someone else first, to find out how things were going. Everyone in the city had heard of the mysterious power possessed by the material, and they were all eager to discover how incapable or stupid his neighbour was.

"I'll send my honest old Prime Minister to the weavers," thought the Emperor. "He's the best one to see what the stuff looks like, for he has plenty of sense and nobody fills his post better than he does."

So off went the honest old Premier to the workshop where the two swindlers sat busy at their empty looms. "Lor' bless my soul!" thought the Minister with eyes starting out of his head. "Why, I can't see anything!" But he was careful not to say so.

The two swindlers begged him to take a closer look—didn't he find the colours and design most attractive? They then pointed to the empty loom but, although the poor old Minister opened his eyes wider and wider. he couldn't see a thing; for there wasn't a thing to see. "Good Lord!" he thought, "Is it possible that I'm stupid? I never suspected that, and not a soul must hear of it. Can it be that I'm unfit for my post? No, it will never do for me to say that I can't see the material."

"Well, what do you think of it?" asked the one who pretended to be weaving.

"Oh, it's charming! Quite exquisite!" said the old Minister, looking through his spectacles. "What a pattern and what colouring! I shall certainly tell the Emperor how pleased I am with it."

"Ah, we're glad to hear that," said the swindlers. and they then gave details of the

colours and the peculiar design. The old
Minister listened carefully, so as to be able
to repeat all this when he came back to the
Emperor—which he duly did.

The swindlers now demanded more money,
more silk and more gold thread, for these
would be required for weaving. They put it
all into their own pockets—not a thread
came into the loom—while they went on
working the empty frames as before.

By and by, the Emperor sent another
honest official to see how the weaving was
getting on and whether the stuff wouldn't
soon be ready. The same thing happened to
him as to the Minister: he looked and
looked but, as nothing was there but the
empty looms, he couldn't see anything.

"There, isn't it a handsome piece!" said
the swindlers, as they pointed out the beauty
of the design which wasn't there at all.

"I know I'm not stupid," thought the man,
"so it must be my fine position I'm not fit
for. Some people might think that rather
funny, but I must take good care they don't
get to hear of it." And then he praised the

material which he couldn't see and assured them of his delight in its charming shades and its beautiful design. "Yes, it's quite exquisite," he said to the Emperor, when he got back.

The splendid material became the talk of the Town. And now the Emperor himself said he must see it while it was still in the loom. Quite a throng of select people, including the two honest old officials who had been there already, went with him to where both the crafty swindlers were now weaving for all they were worth without the vestige of a thread.

"Look, isn't it magnificent!" said the two honest officials. "If your Majesty will but glance—what a pattern, what colouring!" And they pointed to the empty loom, feeling certain that the others could see the material.

"What's this?" thought the Emperor. "I can't see anything—this is appalling! Am I stupid? Am I not fit to be Emperor? This is the most terrible thing that could happen to me ... Oh, it's quite wonderful," he said

to them; "it has our most gracious approval."
And he gave a satisfied nod, as he looked at
the empty loom; he wasn't going to say that
he couldn't see anything. All the courtiers
who had come with him looked and looked,
but they made no more of it than the rest
had done. Still, they all said just what the
Emperor said—"Oh, it's quite wonderful!"
—and they advised him to have some clothes
made from this splendid new material and to
wear them for the first time in the grand procession that was shortly taking place. "Magnificent!" "Delightful!" "Superb!" were the
comments that ran from mouth to mouth;
everyone was so intensely pleased with it.
On each of the swindlers the Emperor be-
stowed a knighthood, with a badge to wear
in his button-hole, and the title of Imperial
Weaver.

On the eve of the procession the swindlers sat up all night with something like
twenty lighted candles. People could see how
busy they were finishing off the Emperor's
new clothes. They pretended to take the stuff
off the loom, they clipped away at the air

with huge scissors, they worked at their needles without thread, and at last they announced: "There! The Emperor's clothes are ready!"

Then the Emperor, with his most distinguished gentlemen-in-waiting, went in person to the weavers, who each put out his arm just as if he were holding something and said: "Here are the Breeches! Here is the Robe! Here is the Mantle!" And so on. "They are all as light as gossamer; you can hardly feel you have anything on—that's just the beauty of them."

"Yes, indeed," answered the gentlemen-in-waiting. But they couldn't see a thing, for there wasn't a thing to see.

"Now will your Imperial Majesty be graciously pleased to take off your clothes?" said the swindlers. "Then we can fit you with the new ones, there in front of the big glass."

So the Emperor took off the clothes he was wearing, and the swindlers pretended to hand him each of the new garments they were supposed to have made, and they took him at the waist as if they were fastening something on ... it was the train, and the Emperor turned and twisted in front of the looking-glass.

"Goodness! How well they suit your Majesty! What a wonderful fit!" they all exclaimed. "What a cut! What colours! What sumptuous robes!"

The Master of Ceremonies came in with an announcement. "The canopy to be carried above your Majesty in the procession is waiting outside."

"All right, I'm ready," said the Emperor. "Aren't they a nice fit!" And he turned round once more in front of the glass, for he really had to make them think he was gazing at his fine clothes.

The chamberlains who were to carry the train groped about on the floor as if they were picking the train up; and, as they walked, they held out their hands, not daring to let it be thought that they couldn't see anything.

There marched the Emperor in the procession under the beautiful canopy, and every-

body in the streets and at the windows said:
"Goodness! The Emperor's new clothes are
the finest he has ever had. What a wonderful train! What a perfect fit!" No one would
let it be thought that he couldn't see anything, because that would have meant he
wasn't fit for his job, or that he was very
stupid. Never had the Emperor's clothes been
such a success.

"But he hasn't got anything on!" said a
little child. "Goodness gracious, do you hear
what the little innocent says?" cried the

father; and the child's remark was whispered from one to the other.

"He hasn't got anything on! There's a little child saying he hasn't got anything on!"

"Well, but he hasn't got anything on!" the people all shouted at last. And the Emperor felt most uncomfortable, for it seemed to him that the people were right. But somehow he thought to himself: "I must go through with it now, procession and all." And he drew himself up still more proudly, while his chamberlains walked after him carrying the train that wasn't there.

THE STAUNCH TIN
SOLDIER

There were once twenty-five tin soldiers, all brothers, for they all came from one old tin spoon. "Shoulder arms! Eyes front!" —that's how they were, and they wore splendid red tunics with blue trousers. The very first thing they ever heard, when the lid was taken off the box in which they were lying, was—"tin soldiers!" It was a little boy who shouted this and clapped his hands. He had been given them for his birthday, and now he was putting them up on the table.

Each soldier was the very image of the other, except for one who was a little bit different. He had only one leg, because he was the last to be made and there wasn't enough tin to go round. Still, there he stood, as firmly on his one leg as the others on their two; and, as it happened, he's the soldier this story is all about.

There were a lot of other toys on the table where the tin soldiers had been put up, but the one you noticed first was a beautiful paper castle; through its tiny windows you could see right into the rooms. In front of it were some small trees standing round a little mirror, which was supposed to represent a lake, with wax swans reflected in it as they swam. Everything was very pretty, and yet the prettiest of all was a little lady who was standing at the open door of the castle. She, too, was cut out of paper, but she was wearing a skirt of the clearest muslin and a narrow blue ribbon draped over her shoulder like a scarf, with a glittering spangle in the middle as big as the whole of her face. The little lady was holding out both her arms; you see, she was a dancer and, besides, she had kicked one of her legs so high in the air that the tin soldier couldn't make out where it was and imagined she only had one leg, like himself.

"That's the wife for me!" he thought to himself. "But she's so grand; she lives in a castle. I've only got a box, and there are twenty-five of us to that; it's no place for her. All the same, I must see if I can't get to know her." Then he lay down at full length behind a snuff-box that was on the table. From here he could keep his eyes on the elegant little lady, who continued to stand on one leg without losing her balance.

Later in the evening, all the other tin soldiers went back into their box, and the people in the house went to bed. The toys now began to play games—visiting, fighting, dancing. The tin soldiers rattled in their box, because they wanted to join in, but they couldn't get the lid off. The nutcrackers turned somersaults, and the slate pencil had

some fun on the slate. There was such a noise
that the canary woke up and began to join in
with some twittering in verse. The only two
who didn't budge were the tin soldier and
the little dancer. She stood perfectly upright
on tiptoe with both arms stretched out, while
he was just as staunch on his one leg; his
eyes never left her for a moment.

Suddenly the clock struck twelve and—
clack! flew the lid from the snuff-box, but
do you suppose there was snuff in it? No,
there was a little black goblin—it was a
kind of Jack-in-the-box.

"Tin soldier!" cried the goblin. "Will you
please keep your eyes to yourself!" But the
tin soldier pretended not to hear.

"All right—you wait till tomorrow!" said
the goblin.

And when tomorrow came and the children
got up, the tin soldier was put away by the
window; and, whether it was the goblin or
the draught that did it, all at once the window flew open and the soldier fell out head
first from the third storey. It was a terrible
fall. There was his leg going straight up in

the air, and he was left standing on his helmet with his bayonet stuck in between the paving-stones.

The maidservant and the little boy came down directly to look for him; but although they very nearly trod on him, they never saw him. If only the tin soldier had called out "Here I am!" they would have found him easily enough; but he didn't think it would be right to shout out, as he was in uniform.

Presently it began raining, more and more heavily, until it was a regular downpour. When it was over, two street-boys came by. "Gosh, look at that!" said one of them. "There's a tin soldier. Let's send him for a sail." So they made a boat out of a news-paper, put the tin soldier aboard, and away he sailed down the gutter with the two boys running alongside and clapping their hands. Bless my soul, how the waves did rock in the gutter, and what a strong current there was! Well, after all, it had been a real soaker. The paper boat bobbed up and down, and now and then it whirled round so fast that

the tin soldier became quite dizzy. But he kept
staunch and never moved a muscle; he looked
straight ahead, and still shouldered arms.

All at once the boat drifted in under a
broad culvert; it was as dark as if he were
in his box.

"I wonder where I'm coming to now," he
thought. "I'll swear it's all the fault of that
goblin. If only the little lady were here in
the boat, it could be twice as dark for all
I'd care!"

Just then a great water-rat appeared, who
lived under the culvert. "Where's your passport?" asked the rat. "Now then, show me
your passport!"

But the tin soldier never said a word and
clutched his gun more tightly than ever. The
boat rushed on, and the rat after it. Ugh!
How it ground its teeth and shouted out to
sticks and straws: "Stop him! Stop him! He
hasn't paid the toll! He hasn't shewn his
passport!"

But the current grew stronger and stronger;
the tin soldier could already see daylight
ahead where the culvert ended. But he could

also hear a roaring sound that might well bring dismay to the bravest man. Just think of it—where the culvert ended, the gutter plunged straight out into a large canal. It was as dangerous for him as it would be for us to sail down a big waterfall.

By now he had come so near that there was no stopping. The boat dashed out, the poor tin soldier held himself as stiffly as he could; no one should say that he had moved an eyelid. The boat spun round three or four times and filled right up with water, until it was bound to sink. The tin soldier was now up to his neck; the boat sank deeper and deeper; the paper grew more and more sodden. At last the water closed over the soldier's head ... He thought of the pretty little dancer whom he would never see again, and the old song rang in his ears:

"On, on, brave warrior!
On, where death awaits thee!"

At this moment, the paper went to pieces, and the tin soldier fell right through—but was instantly swallowed by a large fish. Oh, and how dark it was inside! Even worse than it was in the culvert, and so terribly cramped, too. But the tin soldier was still staunch, still shouldering arms, as he lay at full length.

The fish darted about, making the most terrifying twists and turns. Then at last it lay quite still, a lightning flash went through it, there was broad daylight, and someone called out: "A tin soldier!" The fish had been caught, taken to market and sold, and here it was in the kitchen, where the maid cut it open with a big knife. She picked up the soldier by the waist with her two fingers and carried him into the parlour, where everyone wanted to see this extraordinary man who had been travelling about inside a fish. But the tin soldier thought nothing of it. They set him up on the table, and there—well, what wonderful things can happen! The tin soldier found himself in the very same room as he had been in before. There they were— the same children, the same toys on the table, the same beautiful castle with the pretty little dancer who still stood on one leg and kept the other one high in the air—she, too, had been staunch. This touched the tin soldier, who could have wept tears of tin, only that would hardly have done! He looked at her, and she looked at him, but neither of them spoke.

Suddenly one of the small boys took and threw the soldier straight into the stove. He had no reason for doing this; of course, the Jack-in-the-box was behind it all.

The tin soldier stood in a complete glow; the heat that he felt was tremendous, but whether it came from the actual fire or from love, he had no idea. All his bright colours were gone, but no one could tell if this had happened on his voyage or was the result of grief. He looked at the little lady, she looked at him, and he could feel that he was melting, but he still stood staunchly with arms at the shoulder. Then a door opened, the draught caught the dancer, and she flew like a sylph right into the stove to the tin soldier, flared up in a flame and was gone. The tin soldier was melted down to a lump and, when the maid cleared out the ashes next morning, she found him in the shape of a little tin heart; but all that was left of the dancer was her spangle, and that was burnt as black as coal.

THE FLYING TRUNK

There was once upon a time a merchant, who was so rich that he could pave the whole street, and most of a little alley as well, with silver money. But he didn't do that, because he knew another way of using his money. If he paid out a penny, it brought him in a florin; that's the kind of merchant he was ... And then he died.

All this money now came to his son, and he led a merry life. He went out dancing every night, made paper kites from banknotes and played ducks and drakes on the lake with gold pieces instead of pebbles. Money would soon go that way, and it did. At last he'd only got fourpence left, and nothing to wear but a pair of slippers and an old dressing-gown. His friends had nothing more to do with him now, as of course they couldn't be seen in the street with him; but one of them, who was good-natured, sent him an old trunk, saying, "Pack up!" Yes, that was all very well, but he hadn't got anything to pack, so he got into the trunk himself.

It was a comic sort of trunk. As soon as you pressed the lock, the trunk could fly. And fly it did. It zoomed away with him, up through the chimney, high above the clouds, further and further into the distance. The bottom kept creaking, and he was terrified that it might give way—dear me, that would have been a nice bit of acrobatics! And at last he came to the land of the Turks. He hid the trunk away under some dried leaves in a wood and walked off into the town. It was all right his doing that, for of course all the Turks went about in dressing-gown

and slippers the same as he did. Then he
met a nurse with a baby. "I say, you Turk-
nanny," he began, "what's this great castle
here, close to the town, with the high windows?"

"That's where the King's daughter lives,"
she answered. "It's been foretold her that
she'll have an unhappy love-affair, and so no
one's allowed to visit her without the King
and Queen being there."

"Thank you," said the merchant's son;
and he went back to the wood, got into his
trunk, and flew up on to the castle roof,
where he crawled in through the window to
the Princess.

She was lying on the sofa, asleep. She was
so pretty that the merchant's son felt he must
kiss her. This woke her up, and she was very
frightened, until he told her he was the Turkish
God who had come down to her from the
sky. She liked that very much.

Then they sat beside each other, and he
told her stories about her eyes. They were
the loveliest dark lakes, he said, where her
thoughts went swimming like mermaids. And

he told her stories about her forehead; it was a snowy mountain with the most wonderful rooms and pictures inside it. And he told her about the stork, which brings the dear little babies. Yes, yes, they were lovely stories that he told her. And then he proposed to the Princess, and she at once said yes.

"But you must come here on Saturday," she said. "The King and Queen are coming to tea with me then. They will be so proud of my marrying the Turkish God; only be sure you have a really fine story to tell them, because my father and mother do so enjoy that. My mother likes a story to be goody-goody and correct, but my father likes it to be funny, so that he can laugh."

"All right," he said, "I shan't bring any other wedding present, but simply a story." Then they said goodbye; but the Princess gave him a sword which was decorated with gold coins—and he had plenty of use for those.

So off he flew and bought himself a new dressing-gown; and then he sat in the wood and began to think out a good story. It had to be ready by Saturday and, after all, that's not so easy.

At last he was ready, and Saturday arrived.

The King, the Queen and all the Court were waiting at tea-time with the Princess. They received him most charmingly.

"Now will you tell us a story?" said the Queen. "One that goes deep and has a moral."

"Yes, but one that'll make us laugh, mind you!" said the King.

"Very well," said the merchant's son and began his story. So now we must listen very carefully.

Once upon a time there was a bundle of matches; they were tremendously proud of their high birth. Their family tree—that's to say, the tall fir-tree that each little match-stick came from—had been a huge old tree in the wood. And now the matches lay on the shelf between a tinder-box and an old iron cook-pot, and they told the other two about the time when they were young. "Ah, yes," they said, "in those days, with the velvet moss at our feet, we really were on velvet.

Every morning and evening we had diamond tea; that was the dew. And all day we had sunshine—if there was any sunshine—and all the little birds had to tell us stories. We could see, too, how well off we were, because the broad-leaved trees, they only wore clothes in summer, whereas our family could afford green clothes all the year round. But then the woodcutters arrived; that was the great upheaval, and our family was all split up. Our founder and head was given a place as mainmast on board a splendid ship that could sail round the world if she liked; the other branches went to other places and, as for us, we've got the task of lighting up for the common herd; that's how we gentle-folk come to be in the kitchen."

"Well, things have gone differently with me," said the cook-pot which stood along-side the matches. "Right from the time I first came out into the world, I've been scrubbed and boiled again and again. I've got an eye for the practical and, strictly speaking, I'm No. 1 in this house. My great delight, at a time like after dinner, is to sit clean and tidy on the shelf and have a nice chat with my friends. But except for the water-bucket, who now and then goes down into the yard, we spend all our time indoors. Our one news-bringer is the market basket, but that goes in for a lot of wild talk about the government and the people. Why, the other day there was an elderly jug so flabbergasted by what the basket said that it fell down and broke in pieces. It's an out-and-out radical, that basket, mark my words!"

"How you do chatter!" said the tinder-box; and the steel let fly at the flint, so that it gave out sparks. "Come on, let's have a cheerful evening!"

"Yes, let's discuss who belongs to the best family," said the matches.

"No, I don't like talking about myself," said the earthenware jar. "Let's have a social evening. I'll begin. I'll tell you about the sort of thing that we've all been through; then you can really enter into it, and that makes it so enjoyable. On the shores of the Baltic, where the Danish beech-trees—"

"That's a splendid way to begin," said all

the plates. "Just the kind of story we like!"

"Well, that's where I was brought up, in a quiet family. The furniture was polished, the floor washed, and we had clean curtains every fortnight."

"It does sound interesting the way you tell it," said the broom. "One can hear at once that it's a lady telling the story; there's such a refined note running through it all."

"That's just how I feel," said the bucket, and it gave a little hop of sheer delight, and that meant "splash!" on the floor. Then the cook-pot went on with its story, and the end was every bit as good as the beginning.

The plates all rattled with joy, and the broom took some green parsley out of the bin and crowned the cook-pot with it, knowing this would annoy the others and "if I crown her to-day," she thought, "then she'll crown me to-morrow."

"Now I'm going to dance," said the tongs, and dance she did—my word, what a high kick! The old chintz on the chair in the corner fairly split himself looking at it. "Now may I be crowned?" asked the tongs, and crowned she was.

"After all, they're the merest riff-raff," thought the matches.

The tea-urn was then supposed to give a song, but it had a cold, it said; it could only sing when it was on the boil. It was really just being rather superior; it never would sing except when standing on the table, in there with the master and mistress.

Over in the window lay an old quill pen that the maid generally wrote with. There was nothing remarkable about it except that it had been dipped much too far into the inkpot, but this made it very stuck-up. "If the tea-urn doesn't want to sing," said the quill pen, "then it needn't. In a cage hanging outside is a nightingale—she can sing. It's true she's never had any lessons, but we won't find fault with that this evening."

"I consider it quite out of place," said the tea-kettle, who was the regular kitchen-singer and half-sister to the tea-urn, "that a foreign bird like that should be allowed to sing here.

Is it patriotic? I leave it to the market basket to decide."

"I'm disappointed, that's all," said the market basket. "You've no idea how disappointed I am. Is this a suitable way to spend the evening? Instead of turning the house upside down, wouldn't it be better to put it straight? Then each one would find his proper place, and I should be cock of the walk. Very different to the way things are going now."

"That's it, let's kick up a shindy!" they all exclaimed. Just then the door opened. It was the maid. They all stood still; no one uttered a syllable. But there wasn't a pot among them that didn't know perfectly well how much it could do and how elegant it was. "Yes," they thought, "if we'd wanted, we could easily have turned it into quite a gay evening."

The maid took the matches and struck a light with them—my goodness, how they spluttered and blazed! "Now," thought the matches, "now everyone can see that we are the ones. This is where we shine, where we sparkle!"—and then they burnt right out.

"That was a lovely tale," said the Queen.

"I quite felt myself in the kitchen together with the matches. Yes, thou shalt certainly marry our daughter."

"Ra-ther!" said the King, "thou shalt marry our daughter on Monday." They said "thou" to him now because, you see, he was to be one of the family.

The wedding was all fixed and, the evening before, the whole town was lit up. Cakes and buns were thrown to be scrambled for by the crowd. The street boys stood on tiptoe and shouted hurrah and whistled on their fingers. There were great goings on.

"I suppose I'd better take a hand as well," thought the merchant's son; and so he bought rockets and whizzbangs and every sort of firework you could think of, put them in his trunk and then flew up into the air with them.

Rootsch! How they went off! How they pooffed and popped! The Turks almost jumped out of their skins, and their slippers flew about their ears. Never before had they seen such a vision in the sky. They knew

now that it really was the Turkish God who
was to marry the Princess.

Directly the merchant's son landed in the
wood again with his trunk, he thought, "I
may as well walk into the town and hear
how people have taken it." It was natural
enough that he should want to find that out.

Heavens, the way people talked! Every
single person he asked gave his own version,
but one and all were enchanted.

"I saw the Turkish God himself," said one.
"He had eyes like shining stars, and his
beard was like a foaming torrent."

"He flew off in a mantle of fire," said

another. "I saw the loveliest little cherubs peeping out from the folds."

Yes, they were pretty things he listened to; and tomorrow was his wedding day.

He now went back to the wood to get into his trunk—but where was it? The trunk was burnt right up. The fireworks had left a spark which set fire to the trunk, and this was now in ashes. No more could he fly, no more could he go to his bride.

All day she stood on the roof and waited. She's waiting still—while he goes trudging round the world, telling stories. But they're not so jolly as the one he told about the matches.

WILLIE WINKIE*)
(OLE LUKØJE)

Nobody in the world knows so many stories as Willie Winkie ... And he knows
how to tell them, too—no doubt about that!

Late in the evening, when children are
sitting nice and quietly at a table or on their
stools, that's when Willie Winkie comes
along. He comes ever so softly up the stairs,
for he goes in his stocking-feet, and he very
gently opens the door. Then fft! he squirts
sweet milk into the children's eyes—only
the tiniest drop, yet always enough to stop
them keeping their eyes open—and so they
don't see him. He steals up just behind them

*) The Mother Goose rhyme beginning:
"Wee Willie Winkie runs through the town,—" is almost
as well-known to Danish children as our own, and "Willie
Winkie" is translated and explained to them as 'Ole Lukøje'.

and gently blows down their necks, and then their heads grow heavy. It's all right —it doesn't hurt them, because Willie Winkie is really most kind to children; all he wants is to see them quieten down, and for that it's best to get them to bed. They must be quite still before he can tell them stories.

When at last the children are asleep, Willie Winkie sits down on the bed. He's nicely dressed, and his coat's made of some sort of silk—though it's hard to say what colour it is, for as he turns about it's all shot with green and red and blue. Under each arm he carries an umbrella. One umbrella, with pictures on it, he holds over the good children, so that they have the loveliest dreams all night; and the other umbrella, without anything on it, he holds over the naughty children, so that they sleep like logs and when they wake in the morning haven't dreamt a thing.

Now you shall hear how Willie Winkie came every night for a whole week to a little boy called Hjalmar, and the stories he told him. There are seven stories altogether, for there are seven days in the week.

Monday

"Now look here!" said Willie Winkie one evening, when he had got Hjalmar to bed. "First. I'm going to smarten things up"— and straight away all the flowers in the flower-pots became large trees stretching their long branches up under the ceiling and along the walls, until the whole room was turned into a lovely bower, and all the branches were full of blossom; every flower was prettier than a rose, with a delicious smell, and, if you cared to taste it, was sweeter than jam. The fruit all glistened like gold, and there were buns that were bursting with currants—you never saw anything like it! But all at once there began a most dreadful hullabaloo over in the drawer where Hjalmar kept his school-books.

"What's up now?" said Willie Winkie, as he went over to the table and opened the drawer. It was the slate that was in such distress, because a wrong figure had got into the sum so that it wouldn't come right. The pencil frisked and gambolled at the end of its string like a little dog; it wanted to help the sum, but didn't know how to.

Next, there was a howling set up from inside Hjalmar's copybook—it was simply ghastly to listen to! Running down every page were all the capital letters, each with a small letter beside it, a complete row of them the whole way down. They acted as a copy, and beside them were also some letters which imagined that they looked like the copy ones; Hjalmar had written these, and they straggled about almost as if they had tumbled over the ruled line they were supposed to stand on.

"Look here, this is how you ought to hold

yourselves," said the copy. "Look—sloping a bit like this, with a free swinging stroke."

"Ah, we should so like to," said Hjalmar's letters, "but we can't; we're feeling so bad."

"Then you must have a dose of medicine!" said Willie Winkie.

"Oh, no!" they screamed—and at once stood up as straight as you could wish for.

"There! That's enough story-telling for the present," said Willie Winkie. "Now I must put them through their drill—left, right—left, right!" And he drilled the letters until they stood up as firm and straight as any copy ones. But after Willie Winkie had gone and Hjalmar looked at them the next morning, they were just as miserable-looking as before.

Tuesday

Directly Hjalmar was in bed, Willie Winkie touched all the furniture in the room with his little magic squirt, and they immediately began to chatter. They all chattered about themselves, except the spittoon, which stood in silent annoyance that the others could be so conceited as to talk and think only of themselves and never have a thought for the one who, after all, stood so modestly in the corner and let himself be spat upon.

Over the chest of drawers hung a large painting in a gilt frame. It showed a landscape with tall venerable trees, flowers growing in the meadow, and a great broad stream curving round behind a wood, past many a castle, far out into the open sea.

Willie Winkie touched the painting with his magic squirt, and the birds in it at once began to sing. The branches stirred in the trees, and the clouds scudded along; you could see their shadow drifting over the fields.

Willie Winkie took little Hjalmar and lifted him up to the picture-frame, and Hjalmar put his feet into the picture, right into the tall grass; there he stood, with the sun shining down on him through the branches of the trees. He ran down to the water and got into a little boat that was lying there. It was painted red and white, and its sails shone like silver. Six swans, all with gold crowns down over their necks and a glittering blue star on their heads, towed the boat past the green woods, where the trees were telling tales about robbers and witches, and the flowers had stories of the dear little elves and of all they had heard from the butterflies.

The loveliest fishes, with scales like gold and silver, swam after the boat, leaping up

1 14*

now and then so that there was an answering splash in the water; and the birds flew behind in two long rows, red birds and blue birds, big ones and little ones. The gnats kept dancing round and the cockchafer repeated his "boom! boom"!—they all wanted to go with Hjalmar, and each of them had a story to tell.

Yes, it was a wonderful sail they went for. At one moment the woods were quite thick and dark, and then suddenly they were like a beautiful garden with flowers and sunshine, and there appeared great castles of glass and marble with princesses on the balconies who were all little girls that Hjalmar knew well and had played with. They reached out their hands, and each one was holding the nicest sugar-pig any sweet-shop could sell. Hjalmar caught hold of one end of a sugar-pig as he sailed past, and the princess held on tight to the other, so they each got a piece; she got the smallest and Hjalmar much the biggest. Little princes, with gold swords carried at the salute, were on guard at every castle, and they showered him with toffee and tin soldiers; they were proper princes!

Sometimes Hjalmar was sailing through forests, and sometimes through what seemed to be immense halls or through the middle of a town. In this way he came to the home of the nurse who had looked after him when he was quite small. She had been so very fond of him, and now she nodded and waved her hand, singing the pretty verses she had made up herself and sent to Hjalmar.

Of you, dear Hjalmar, I often think
    and how as a babe I kissed you
on forehead and mouth and cheek so pink—
    my darling, how much I've missed you!
Your earliest words I heard you crow,
    but soon from your side was driven.
God grant you his blessing here below,
    sweet messenger sent from heaven!

And all the birds joined in her song; the flowers danced on their stalks, and the old trees nodded, just as if Willie Winkie were telling them stories too.

213

Wednesday

Goodness! how the rain was coming down outside! Hjalmar could hear it in his sleep, and when Willie Winkie opened a window. the water came right up to the sill. There was a complete lake outside, but a splendid-looking ship lay alongside the house.

"Hjalmar, my boy, will you come for a sail?" asked Willie Winkie. "Then you'll be able to go off to foreign parts to-night and be back again in the morning."

And all of a sudden Hjalmar found himself standing in his Sunday best on board the splendid ship, and the weather at once became fine. She sailed through the streets,

214

cruised round the church and finally came
out into open sea. On and on they sailed,
until the land was quite out of sight; and
they came upon a flock of storks, who were
also leaving home and were bound for the
warm countries. They were flying one behind
the other and had already flown a very
long way. One of the storks was so tired that
his wings could hardly bear him up any
longer; he was the very last in the row, and
he soon got a long way behind. Finally he
sank with outspread wings lower and lower;
he gave a few more beats with his wings, but
that was no good; and then his feet touched
the ship's rigging, he glided down the sail
and plomp! there he was on the deck.

Then the ship's boy picked him up and
put him in the hen-coop among hens, ducks
and turkeys. The poor stork looked so sorry
for himself amongst them.

"What a creature!" said all the hens.

And the turkey-cock puffed himself out as
big as he could and asked who he was, and
the ducks waddled backwards and nudged
each other—"Quick, get quacking!"

215

Then the stork told about the warmth of Africa, and the pyramids, and the ostrich that ran like a wild horse through the desert; but the ducks never understood what he was saying and so they nudged each other again —"We all agree, don't we, that he's a stupid?"

"As stupid as can be!" said the turkey-cock with a gobble-gobble. At that the stork kept silent and thought about his beloved Africa.

"Those are nice lanky legs you have," said the turkey. "How much a yard?"

"Quack, quack, quack!" chuckled the ducks. But the stork pretended not to hear.

"You may as well join in the laugh", said the turkey to him; "it was very neatly put. Or was it perhaps too low for him? Heigh-ho! He's a bit one-eyed; we must look to ourselves, if we want to have some fun." And they clucked away, and the ducks kept quack-quack-quacking—it was terrible how funny they seemed to think it was.

But Hjalmar went over to the hen-coop, opened the door and called to the stork, who then hopped out on to the deck. He had now had a good rest and seemed to give Hjalmar a nod, in order to thank him. The next moment he spread out his wings and flew off to the warm countries. But the hens went on clucking and the ducks went on quacking, while the turkey-cock became quite red in the face.

"To-morrow we shall make soup of you!" said Hjalmar—and then he woke up. There he was, lying in his little bed. It really was an astonishing voyage Willie Winkie had arranged for him that night.

Thursday

"What do you think I've got here?" said Willie Winkie. "Now don't get frightened; I'm going to show you a little mouse"— and there was the dainty little creature in Willie Winkie's hand as he held it out to him. "It has come," he said, "to invite you to a wedding. There are two little mice here tonight who are entering into matrimony. They live down under the floor of your mother's larder; it ought to be a charming affair".

"But how am I to get through the tiny mousehole in the floor?" asked Hjalmar.

"Leave that to me," said Willie Winkie; "I know how to make you small enough." And he touched Hjalmar with his magic squirt, so that he at once became smaller and smaller

218

and at last was no bigger than your finger. "Now we can borrow the tin soldier's clothes; I think they'll fit you, and it looks so smart to be wearing uniform at a party."

"Ra-ther!" said Hjalmar, and the next moment there he was dressed as the most dapper-looking tin soldier.

"If you'll kindly take a seat in your mother's thimble," said the little mouse, "I'll do myself the honour of pulling you along."

"Good gracious! Miss Mouse," said Hjalmar, "to think of me giving you all that trouble!" And off they drove to the mouse-wedding.

First, they made their way in under the floor by a long passage that was just high enough, and no more, for them to be able to drive along in a thimble, and the whole passage was lit up by touchwood.

"Doesn't it smell nice!" said the mouse that was pulling him. "The whole passage has been rubbed with bacon-rind; there's nothing to touch it!"

Now they entered the wedding-chamber. To the right stood all the little she-mice,

219

twittering and tittering as if they were making fun of each other; to the left stood all the he-mice, stroking their whiskers with their paws. But out in the middle of the floor were the bridal pair, standing in a scooped-out cheese and kissing each other like anything in front of everybody. Well, after all, they were engaged and were going to be married almost at once.

More and more guests kept arriving, and the mice looked like trampling each other to death. The bride and bridegroom had stationed themselves in the middle of the doorway, so there was no getting either out or in. The whole room, like the passage, had been rubbed with bacon-rind, which was all the refreshment there was; but for dessert there was produced a pea in which a mouse belonging to the family had nibbled the name of the bridal pair—or rather, the first letter. That was considered something altogether out of the ordinary.

All the mice agreed that it was a lovely wedding and that they had talked with such interesting people.

Finally, Hjalmar drove home again. He had certainly been in very smart society; on the other hand, he had had to put up with no end of a shrinking, to make himself small enough to get into a tin soldier's uniform.

Friday

"You'd never believe how many elderly people would like to get hold of me," said Willie Winkie. "Especially the ones who've done something they shouldn't. 'Dear, kind Winkie', they say to me, 'We can't shut our eyes at night, and so we lie awake and see our evil deeds sitting on the edge of the bed like hideous little goblins and squirting us with hot water. Do come and chase them away, so that we can get a good sleep!' And then they add with a deep sigh, 'We're only too glad to pay. Good-night, Winkie—the

222

money's in the window'. But I don't do it for money," said Willie Winkie.

"Now, what are we going to have tonight?" asked Hjalmar.

"Well, I don't know if you'd care to go to another wedding—quite a different sort to yesterday's, I may say. Your sister's big doll—the one that looks like a man and is called Herman—is to marry the doll Bertha; and, as it's Bertha's birthday, there will be a lot of presents."

"Yes, I know what that means!" said Hjalmar. "Whenever the dolls want new clothes, my sister lets them have a birthday or a wedding. That must have happened a hundred times."

"Well, but to-night's wedding is the 101st time, and when Number 101 is over there won't be any more. That's why it's going to be so brilliant. Just look!"

And Hjalmar looked across at the table. There stood the little cardboard house with lights in the windows, and all the tin soldiers were presenting arms outside. The bride and bridegroom were seated on the floor, leaning

223

up against the leg of the table and looking very thoughtful, as indeed they might well do. But Willie Winkie draped himself in Grannie's black petticoat and married them! When the wedding was over, all the furniture in the room joined in singing the following beautiful song, which had been written by the pencil and went to the tune of the devil's tattoo:—

Our song shall greet like wind and weather
these two that the priest has tied together;
so poker-stiff they stand in tether,
each of them made of chamois leather!
  Hurrah for bride and groom together!
  Hurrah for them both in wind and
                                  weather!

Next came the wedding presents; they had said they would rather not have any eatables, as their love was enough for them to live on.

"Which do you think?" said the bridegroom to his bride. "Shall we go and stay in the country, or shall we travel abroad?" They asked advice of the swallow, who was a great traveller, and of the old hen, who

224

had hatched five broods of chicks. The swallow described the lovely warm countries, where the grapes hang in big heavy bunches and the air is so soft and the colour on the hills is something quite unknown to us here.

"Still, they haven't got our garden cabbage!" said the hen. "I once spent the summer with all my chicks in the country; there was a gravel pit we could go and scratch in, and then we had the use of a garden where there were cabbages—such a green, they were! I can't imagine anything lovelier."

"But one cabbage-stalk looks just like another," said the swallow. "And then again, the weather here is so often bad."

"Oh, well, we're used to that," replied the hen.

"But it's so cold. It freezes."

"That just suits the cabbages," said the hen. "Besides, we get warm weather too, sometimes. Don't you remember, only four years ago, we had a summer that lasted five weeks! It was so hot here that you could hardly breathe ... And then we don't get all those poisonous creatures they have abroad; and we are free from brigands. Anyone who doesn't think our country is the best of all is a scoundrel; he doesn't really deserve to live here"—and tears came into the hen's eyes. "I've done a bit of travelling myself," she added. "I've ridden over 50 miles in a coop. There's no fun at all in travel."

"Yes, the hen's a sensible woman," said the doll Bertha. "I don't want to go mountaineering either. It only means that first you go up and—then you go down. No, let's move out to the gravel pit and go for a walk in the cabbage patch."

And that's how they left it.

Saturday

"Any stories for me to-night?" asked little Hjalmar, as soon as Willie Winkie had got him to bed.

"We haven't time for that this evening," said Winkie, as he opened above him the umbrella with the prettiest pictures on. "Take a peep at those Chinese!"—and the whole umbrella looked like a great Chinese bowl with blue trees and bridges with pointed arches, where there were little Chinese who stood nodding their heads.

"We must have everything trim and tidy

for tomorrow," said Winkie. "You see, it's a holy day; it's Sunday. I must go up the church-tower and see if the little church-elves are cleaning the bells, so that they ring out nicely. I must get along to the fields and see if the breezes are blowing the dust off the grass and the leaves. And then—what is really my hardest task—I must have all the stars down and give them a thorough polish. I take them into my apron; but, first, each one of them has to be numbered, and the holes they fit into up there must also be numbered, so that they can find their right places again; otherwise, they wouldn't fit tight and we should get too many shooting stars, as they dropped out one after the other."

"I say, look here, Mr. Winkie," said an old portrait hanging on the wall of Hjalmar's bedroom. "I'm Hjalmar's great-grandfather. Thank you for telling the boy these stories, but you mustn't muddle him with wrong ideas. The stars can't be taken down and polished. A star is a globe, the same as the earth is; that's just the beauty of it."

"Thanks very much, old great-grand-

228

father!" said Willie Winkie. "Thanks very much! You're of course the head of the family—the Grand Old Man—but I'm older than you are. I'm an ancient heathen —the Romans and Greeks call me the Dream God. I visit the very best houses, continually, and I know how to get on with all sorts, both young and old. Now you can tell a story of your own." And Willie Winkie picked up his umbrella and away he went.

"Dear, dear!" said the old portrait. "One mayn't even express one's opinion nowadays."

And at that moment Hjalmar woke up.

Sunday

"Good evening," said Willie Winkie, and Hjalmar nodded; but then he jumped up and turned his great-grandfather's portrait with its face to the wall, so that it shouldn't butt into the conversation as it did the day before.

"Please tell me some stories: the one about the five peas that lived in a pod, and the one about the cock-a-doodle-doo that made love to the hen-a-doodle-doo, and the one about the darning-needle who was so stuck-up that she fancied she was a sewing-needle!"

230

"Ah, but one can have too much of a good thing," said Willie Winkie. "I'd rather show you something. I tell you what, I'll show you my brother. He never comes to anyone more than once and, when he comes, he takes them up on his horse and tells them stories. He only knows two: one is so utterly beautiful that no one on earth can imagine it, and the other is so ghastly and terrible—well, it's impossible to describe it."

Then Willie Winkie lifted little Hjalmar up to the window and said, "Look, there's my brother. He's also called Death. You see, he's nothing like so horrid to look at as he is in pictures, where he's nothing but a skeleton. No, he has silver lace on his tunic—it's a splendid hussar uniform with a black velvet cloak flying behind him over his horse. Look how he gallops along!"

And Hjalmar saw how this other Winkie rode away, taking both young and old up on his horse. Some he placed in front of him, others behind; but he always asked them first, "What does it say in your report?" "Good," they all answered. "Ah, but let me see it myself", he said. Then they had to show him the report, and all the ones who had "very good" or "excellent" came to the front seat on the horse and were told the beautiful story. But those who had "moderate" or "poor" had to sit behind and hear the terrible story; they trembled and wept and tried to jump off the horse, but they couldn't do that because they had immediately grown fast on to it.

"But Death is a most wonderful Willie Winkie," said Hjalmar. "I'm not a bit afraid of him."

"No, and you needn't be," said Willie Winkie, "Mind you get a good report, that's all."

"Most instructive!" muttered the great grandfather's portrait. "It does some good, after all, to express one's opinion." And he was quite contented.

There! That's the story of Willie Winkie. Now this evening he can tell you some more himself.

THE SWINEHERD

Once upon a time there was a prince who hadn't much money, but he had a kingdom; and though this was quite small, it was large enough to marry on, and marry he would.

Still, it was really rather bold of him to say straight out to the Emperor's daughter; "Will you have me"? But sure enough he did, for his name was famous everywhere, and there were hundreds of princesses who would only too gladly have taken him. But do you think she did? Well, now just listen. Growing on the grave of the Prince's father was a rose-tree—oh, such a lovely rose-tree. It only flowered every five years, and even then had but one solitary bloom. But this rose smelt so sweet that it made you forget all your cares and troubles. And the Prince also had a nightingale that could sing just as if it had all the loveliest tunes hidden away in its little throat. The Princess should have both the rose and the nightingale, he said; and so they were placed in big silver caskets and sent to her.

The Emperor had them brought before him in the great hall, where the Princess was playing "visitors" with her maids-of-honour. They never did anything else and, when she saw the big caskets with the presents inside, she clapped her hands with glee.

"I do hope it's a pussy-cat", she said ... But then out came the lovely rose.

"Oh, isn't it pretty!" cried all the maids-of-honour.

"It's more than pretty," said the Emperor, "it's handsome."

But when the Princess touched it she nearly burst into tears. "Oh, Papa, what a shame!" she cried. "It's not artificial, it's real!"

"What a shame!" repeated all the court-ladies. "It's real!"

"Come, let's first see what's in the other casket before we get annoyed," suggested the Emperor. And then out came the nightingale. Its singing was so lovely that for the moment there wasn't a thing that could be said against it.

"Superbe! Charmant!" exclaimed the maids-of-honour, for they all talked French, the one worse than the other. "How the bird reminds me of Her late Majesty's musical-box!" said an old courtier. "Dear me, yes! Exactly the same tone, the same expression!"

"So it is," said the Emperor; and he cried like a child.

"All the same, I can't believe that it's real," said the Princess.

"Yes, it is; it's a real live bird," said the ones who had brought it.

"All right, then let it fly away," said the

Princess, and she wouldn't hear of the Prince being allowed to come.

But he wasn't going to be put off like that. He smeared his face with brown and black, pulled his cap down over his eyes and knocked at the door. "Good morning, Emperor!" he said. "I wonder if you've got a job for me here at the Castle."

"Ah, well," said the Emperor, "there are so many come and ask that. But now, let me see—yes, I want some one to mind the pigs. We've such a lot of pigs."

And so the Prince was appointed Imperial Swineherd. He was given a miserable little room down by the pig-sties, and there he had to live. But all day he sat working, and by the evening he had made a lovely little pot with bells round it and, as soon as the pot boiled, these tinkled charmingly; they played the old tune of—.

"Ah, my dear Augustine,
our dreams are all done, done, done!"

But the cunningest arrangement of all was that, if you held your finger in the steam from the pot, you could at once smell what was being cooked on every fire in the town. Well, of course, that was something quite different from a rose.

Presently the Princess came strolling along with all her court-ladies, and when she heard the music she stopped, looking so delighted; for she, too, could play "Ah, my dear Augustine"—it was the only tune she knew, and she played it with one finger.

"Why, that's *my* tune!" she said. "This pigman must be a man of taste. Look here, go in and ask him how much he wants for the instrument."

So one of the court-ladies had to run in and see him; but she put on her clogs first.

"How much do you want for that pot?" she asked.

"I want ten kisses from the Princess," answered the pigman.

"Goodness gracious!" said the maid-of-honour.

"That's the price; I can't take less," said the pigman.

"Well, what does he say?" asked the Princess.

"I really can't repeat it," said the maid-of-honour. "It's too dreadful."

"Well, then, whisper it"—and the maid-of-honour whispered it.

"Oh, how rude he is!" said the Princess and walked off at once. But when she had gone a little way, the bells began to tinkle so charmingly—

"Ah, my dear Augustine,
our dreams are all done, done, done!"

"Come," said the Princess, "ask him if he will take ten kisses from my ladies-in-waiting."

"No, thank you," said the pigman. "Ten kisses from the Princess, or I stick to my pot!"

"How horribly annoying!" said the Princess. "Well, then, you ladies 'll have to stand in front of me, so that no one can see."

The court-ladies went and stood in front of her, spreading out their dresses; and then the pigman had his ten kisses and she got her pot.

Goodness! What fun they had! Day and night the pot was kept on the boil. There wasn't a kitchen in the town where they didn't know what was being cooked, whether it was the Mayor's or the shoemaker's. The maids-of-honour danced about, clapping their hands with glee.

"We know who's going to have soup and pancakes, and we know who's going to have chops and jelly. It's so interesting."

"Most interesting," observed the High Stewardess.

"Yes, but not a word to anyone, mind you; for I'm the Emperor's daughter."

"O dear, no!" they all replied. "We shouldn't dream of it."

The swineherd—that is to say, the Prince, but you see, they didn't know but what he was a regular pigman—couldn't let the day go by without making something. The next thing he made was a rattle. When you swung it round, it played all the waltzes and jigs and polkas that anybody had ever heard of.

"Now that really is *superbe*," said the Princess, as she was passing. "I've never

heard anything lovelier. Look here, go in and ask him what he wants for that instrument. But, mind, no kisses!"

"He wants a hundred kisses from the Princess," said the lady-in-waiting who had been in to ask.

"The fellow must be mad," said the Princess and began to walk off. But when she had gone a little way, she stopped. "Art must be encouraged," she said; "after all, I'm the Emperor's daughter. Tell him he shall have ten kisses like yesterday, and my ladies-in-waiting will give him the rest."

"Oh, but we couldn't bear to do that," said the ladies.

"Nonsense!" said the Princess. "If I can kiss him, so can you. Remember, I give you wages and board"—and once more the maid-of-honour had to go in and see the pig-man.

"A hundred kisses from the Princess," he said, "or we stay as we are."

"Stand in front!" she cried. And so all the court-ladies placed themselves in front, and the kissing began.

242

"What on earth are they all up to over there by the sties?" said the Emperor, who had just stepped out on to his balcony. He rubbed his eyes and put on his spectacles. "Why, it's the ladies-in-waiting, up to some game or other. Perhaps I'd better go and have a look"—and he gave a hitch to the back of his slippers, for he had trodden them down at the heel.

Phew! What a hurry he was in!

As soon as he came down into the courtyard, he crept along very quietly. And the maids-of-honour were so busy counting the kisses, for it had to be fair do's—he mustn't have too many kisses, nor yet too few—that they never noticed the Emperor, who now drew himself up on tiptoe.

"What's all this?" he said, when he saw them kissing; and he slogged them over the head with his slipper, just as the young pigman was having his eighty-sixth kiss. "Out you get!" said the Emperor, for he was furious, and both Princess and swineherd were turned out of his kingdom.

Look, there she sat crying, while the swine-

herd scolded and the rain came down in torrents.

"Poor me!" said the Princess. "If only I had accepted the handsome Prince! Oh, I am so unhappy!"

The swineherd went behind a tree, wiped off the black and brown from his face, threw away his old clothes and now stepped forward in princely robes that were so magnificent that the Princess couldn't help making a curtsey.

244

"My dear, I've come to despise you," he said. "An honest prince you rejected. The rose and the nightingale were not to your taste. But the swineherd—you could kiss him for the sake of a musical box. Now you can have what you asked for!"

And with that he went into his kingdom, shut the door and bolted it; but she could stand outside if she cared to and sing—

"Ah, my dear Augustine,
our dreams are all done, done, done!"

THE NIGHTINGALE

You know of course that in China the Emperor is a Chinese and his subjects are Chinese too. The story I'm going to tell you happened many years ago, but that's just why you had better hear it now before it's forgotten.

The Emperor's palace was the finest palace in the world, made entirely of delicate porcelain. It was all so precious and fragile that you had to be tremendously careful how you touched anything. The garden was full of the rarest flowers, and the loveliest of

246

these had little silver bells tied to them which tinkled so that no one should go by without noticing them. Yes, everything in the Emperor's garden was most carefully thought out, and it stretched so far that even the gardener had no idea where it ended. If you kept on walking, you found yourself in a glorious wood with tall trees and deep lakes. The wood went right down to the sea, which was blue and deep; big ships could sail right in under the branches of the trees. Here lived a nightingale that sang so beautifully that even the poor fisherman, who had so much else to see to, would stop and listen, when he was taking his nets in at night and suddenly heard the nightingale. "My word! that's lovely!" he said; but then he had to get on with his work and forgot about the bird. Yet when she sang again the following night and the fisherman was out there with his nets, "My word!" he repeated, "that is lovely!"

From every country in the world travellers came and marvelled at the Emperor's great city, his palace and his garden; but as soon as they heard the nightingale, everyone said the same—"Oh, but that's the best of all!" And when they got home from their travels, they had many tales to tell, and clever people wrote books about the city and the palace and the garden, yet they never forgot the nightingale; she was given the place of honour. And the poets wrote the most lovely poems, all about the nightingale in the wood there beside the deep sea.

These books went all over the world, and so in course of time some of them reached the Emperor. There he sat in his golden chair, reading and reading; and now and then he nodded his head, for he was pleased to come across such splendid descriptions of the city and the palace and the garden. "But the nightingale is really the best of all", said the book he was reading.

"What's this?" thought the Emperor. "The nightingale? Why, I've never heard of her! Is there such a bird in my Empire and, what's more, in my own garden? Nobody's ever told me that—one has to read about it in a book!" And, with that, he summoned his gentleman-in-waiting, who was so grand that, whenever anyone of lower rank than himself ventured to speak to him or to ask a question, he only answered "P!"—and that means nothing at all.

"It says here that we have a most remarkable bird called a nightingale", said the Emperor. "They declare that there's nothing like her in all my Empire. Why have I never been told of this before?"

"It's the first I've ever heard of her," answered the gentleman-in-waiting. "She's never been presented at Court."

"I command her to be brought here this evening to sing to me," said the Emperor. "The whole world knows what I possess— and I know nothing!"

"It's the first I've ever heard of her," repeated the gentleman-in-waiting. "I shall look for her, and I shall find her."

Find her? But where? The gentleman-in-waiting ran upstairs and downstairs, through rooms and passages, but none of the people he met had ever heard of the nightingale. So the gentleman-in-waiting hurried once more to the Emperor and said it was obviously a story invented by those who write books. "Your Majesty mustn't believe everything you read. Most of it's just made up—what they call the black art."

"But the book I read it in," said the Emperor, "was sent me by the high and mighty Emperor of Japan, so it can't be untrue. I *will* hear the nightingale. She's to come and sing to-night, under my royal patronage; and if she fails to appear, then every courtier shall be punched in the stomach directly after supper."

"Tsing-pe!" said the gentleman-in-waiting and ran up and down all the stairs again, through all the rooms and passages; half the Court ran with him, for they didn't a bit like the idea of being punched in the stomach. They kept asking after this extraordinary nightingale that everybody knew about except the people at Court.

At last they came across a poor little girl in the kitchen, who said "Oh, golly—the nightingale? I know her well. My, how she can sing! Every evening I'm allowed to take home a few scraps from the table for my poor sick mother who lives down by the shore; and on my way back I often take a rest in the wood, and then I hear the nightingale singing. It brings tears to my eyes, just as if my mother were kissing me."

"Little kitchen-maid," said the gentleman-in-waiting, "you shall have a regular situation in the kitchen and be allowed to watch the Emperor eating his dinner, if only you'll take us to the nightingale. You see, she's to give a command performance this evening before the Emperor."

So then they all set out for the wood where the nightingale used to sing; half the Court joined in the quest. As they were going along, a cow began to moo. "Ah, there she is!" said the courtiers. "What remarkable strength in such a small creature! Yes, it's certainly not the first time we've heard her."

"No, but that's a cow mooing," said the little kitchen-maid. "We've still got a long way to go."

Then some frogs started croaking in the pond. "Delightful!" said the Emperor's chaplain. "Now I can hear her: just like little church-bells."

"No, those are frogs," said the little kitchen-maid. "But I expect we shall soon hear her now". And then the nightingale began to sing.

"There she is!" said the little girl. "Listen, listen! There she is, up there"—and she pointed to a little grey bird up in the branches.

"Is it possible?" said the gentleman-in-waiting. "Why, I never pictured her like that. How ordinary she looks! I expect she's off colour through having so many distinguished visitors."

"Little nightingale," called out the small kitchen-maid quite boldly, "our gracious Emperor would like you to sing to him."

"With the greatest of pleasure," said the nightingale, and at once began to sing most deliciously.

"Just like glass bells," observed the gentleman-in-waiting. "And look at the way her little throat keeps working. I can't make out why we've never heard her before. She'll make a great hit at Court."

"Shall I sing once more to the Emperor?" asked the nightingale, for she thought the Emperor was there.

"My excellent little nightingale," replied the gentleman-in-waiting, "it is my very pleasant duty to summon you to a concert this evening at the palace. where you will enchant His Imperial Majesty with your delightful singing."

"It sounds best out in the open," said the nightingale. Still, she went along readily enough on hearing it was the Emperor's wish.

At the palace everything had been polished up, until the china walls and floors glittered in the light of thousands and thousands of gold lamps. The loveliest flowers, hung ready for tinkling, were arranged in the corridors; and there was such a draught from the scurrying to and fro that their bells were all set ringing and you couldn't hear a word that was spoken.

In the middle of the great hall in which the Emperor sat was a golden perch for the nightingale. The entire Court was present; and the little kitchen-maid was allowed to stand behind the door, as she now ranked as a regular palace kitchen-maid. Everyone was dressed in their finest clothes, and they all looked at the little grey bird as the Emperor nodded to her to begin.

And the nightingale sang so beautifully that tears came into the Emperor's eyes and trickled right down his cheeks; and then the nightingale's singing became even lovelier— it went straight to his heart. And the Emperor was so pleased that he said the nightingale should have his gold slipper to wear round her neck; but the nightingale said no thank you, she had been rewarded enough already. "I've seen tears in the Emperor''s eyes; that's my richest reward. There's a strange power in an Emperor's tears. Heaven knows, they are reward enough!" And then the nightingale let them hear her lovely voice again.

"Who ever saw such airs and graces!" said the ladies around; and they went and filled their mouths with water so as to gurgle when anyone spoke to them; yes, they thought they could be nightingales too. Even the lackeys and lady's maids expressed their approval; and that's saying a good deal, for they are the most difficult of all to satisfy. There's no doubt whatever, the nightingale made a great hit.

She was now to remain at Court and have her own cage, with leave to go out for two walks in the daytime and one at night. She was given twelve attendants, who each held on tightly to a silk ribbon fastened round her leg. There was absolutely no fun in a walk like that.

The whole city was talking of this remarkable bird, and, when two people met, one of them merely said "night" and the other "gale", and after that they sighed and quite understood each other. What's more, eleven grocers' children were named after her, but not one of them had a note in its head ...

One day a large parcel arrived for the Emperor, with the word "Nightingale" written on the outside.

"I expect this is a new book about our famous bird," said the Emperor. But it wasn't a book at all; it was a little gadget lying in a box—an artificial nightingale that was supposed to look like the live one but was covered all over with diamonds, rubies and sapphires. You only had to wind it up, and it could sing one of the songs that the real nightingale sang; and all the while its tail went up and down, glittering with silver and gold. Round its neck was a little ribbon, on which was written: "The Emperor of Japan's nightingale is poor beside the Emperor of China's."

"How delightful!" they all said; and the one who brought the artificial bird was at once given the title of Chief Imperial Nightingale Bringer.

"Now they must both sing at once,"suggested somebody. "What a duet that will be!"

So the two birds had to sing together; but it wasn't a success, because the real nightingale sang in her own way, whereas the artificial bird went by clockwork. "It can't be blamed for that", said the Master of the Emperor's Music. "It keeps perfect time and follows my own methods exactly." After that, the artificial bird had to sing by itself.

It was just as popular as the real one, and of course it was also much prettier to look at, glittering there like a cluster of brooches and bracelets.

Over and over again it sang its one and only song — thirty-three times without tiring —and the listeners would have liked to hear it all once more, but the Emperor thought that now it was time for the real nightingale to do some singing ... But where ever was she? No one had noticed her fly out of the open window, away to her own green woods.

"Bless my soul, what's the meaning of this?" said the Emperor; and all the courtiers were highly indignant and said what an ungrateful creature the nightingale was. "Still, we've got the best one," they added; and then the artificial bird was obliged to sing once more. That was the thirty-fourth time they were hearing the same song; but they didn't quite know it even yet, for it was so difficult. And the Master of Music gave the bird extraordinary praise; in fact, he declared that it was better than the real nightingale, not merely because of its outward appearance and all the wonderful diamonds, but also for the works inside.

"You see, ladies and gentlemen and, above all, Your Imperial Majesty, with the real nightingale there's no telling what's going to happen. But with the artificial bird everything is fixed beforehand. Such-and-such will be heard and no other. One can account for it all: one can open it up and show the human mind at work, the position of the cylinders, how they go round, and the way in which one thing follows from another!"

Everyone said that they quite agreed, and the Master of Music got permission to show the bird to the public on the following Sunday. "They must also hear it sing," said the Emperor. And hear it they did. They were as delighted as if they had drunk themselves merry on tea—and that's so like the Chinese! They all said "Oh!" and held up one finger—the finger we call "lick-pot"—and nodded their heads. But the poor fisherman who had heard the real nightingale said: "It don't sound so bad—quite like the bird—and yet there's something kind o' missing."

The real nightingale was sent into exile—banished from land and realm. The artificial bird had its place on a silk cushion close to the Emperor's bed; all the presents it had been given, gold and precious stones, lay round about, and it was promoted to be Chief Imperial Bedside Minstrel of the First Class on the Left; for the Emperor considered the side on which the heart lies to be the most distinguished, and even an Emperor has his heart on the left. The Master of Music wrote a book in twenty-five volumes about the mechanical bird; it was very long and learned, full of the most difficult Chinese words, and everyone pretended they had read it and understood it, or else of course they would have been thought stupid and got punched in the stomach.

Well, this went on for a whole year, until the Emperor, his Court and all the other Chinese knew by heart every little gurgle in the throat of the artificial songbird; but for that very reason they came to like it all the better. They could join in the singing themselves, and they did. The street-boys sang "zee-zee-zee, kloo-kloo-klook!" and the Emperor sang it, too! It really was tremendous fun.

But one evening, just as the artificial bird was in full song and the Emperor lay listening in bed, something went "snap!" inside the bird. Then there was a "whirrrrr"; the wheels all went whizzing round ... and the music stopped.

The Emperor quickly jumped out of bed and sent for the doctor, but what could he do? Then they brought along the watchmaker, and after a great deal of talk and poking about he got the bird to work after a fashion; but he said that it mustn't be used too often, as the bearings were almost worn out and it was impossible to get fresh parts that would fit in properly with the music. This was a sad disappointment. Once a year only was the artificial bird allowed to sing, and even that was something of a strain; but on these occasions the Master of Music made a little speech full of difficult words, saying that the bird was just as good as ever—and so of course it was just as good as ever.

Five years had now gone by, and presently the whole country was filled with sorrow, for really in their hearts they were all fond of their Emperor; but now he was ill and not likely to live, it was said. A new Emperor had already been chosen, and people stood out in the street and asked the gentleman-in-waiting how their Emperor was. "P!" he replied and shook his head.

Cold and pale lay the Emperor in his magnificent great bed. The whole Court believed him to be dead, and each of them hastened to pay their respects to the new Emperor. The valets ran out to gossip about it, and the palace housemaids had a large tea-party. Everywhere, in all the rooms and corridors, heavy cloth had been laid down in order to deaden the sound of footsteps; the whole palace was as still as still could be.

But the Emperor wasn't dead yet. Stiff and pale he lay in the magnificent bed with its long velvet curtains and heavy gold tassels; through an open window high up on the wall the moon was shining down on the Emperor and the artificial bird.

The poor Emperor could scarcely breathe; it was just as if something was sitting on his chest. He opened his eyes, and then he saw it was Death that sat on his chest and had put on his gold crown and was holding the Emperor's gold sword in one hand and his splendid banner in the other. All round the bed, from the folds in the great velvet curtains, strange faces were peering, some of them hideous, others wonderfully gentle and kind. They were the Emperor's good and evil deeds, gazing down on him now that Death was sitting on his heart.

"Do you remember that?" they whispered, one after the other. "Do you remember that?" And they told him so much that the sweat stood out on his forehead.

"I never realised that", said the Emperor. "Music, music! Sound the great Chinese drum," he cried, "to save me from hearing what they say!"

But still they went on, and Death kept nodding like a Chinese at every word they whispered.

"Music, music!" shrieked the Emperor.

263

"You wonderful little golden bird, sing, I implore you, sing! I've given you gold and precious stones, I've hung my own gold slipper round your neck—sing, I implore you, sing!"

But the bird was silent; there was no one to wind it up, and it couldn't sing without that. But Death went on staring at the Emperor with his great hollow eyes, and everything was so still, so terribly still.

All at once, close to the window, came a burst of most beautiful singing. It was the little live nightingale, perched in a tree outside. She had heard of her Emperor's distress and had therefore come to sing him consolation and hope; and, as she sang, the shapes grew fainter and fainter, the blood in the Emperor's weak limbs ran faster and faster, and Death himself listened and said, "Go on, little nightingale, go on!"

"Yes, if you'll give me the fine gold sword ... if you'll give me the splendid banner ... if you'll give me the Emperor's crown!"

And Death gave up each treasure for a song, and still the nightingale went on sing-

264

ing. She sang of the quiet churchyard where the white roses bloom, where the elder-tree smells so sweet, and where the fresh grass is watered with the tears of those who are left behind. Then Death began to long for his garden and floated like a cold white mist out of the window.

"Thank you, thank you!" said the Emperor. "You heavenly little bird, now I know who you are! I banished you from land and realm—and yet you have sung those evil visions away from my bed, you have lifted Death from my heart. How can I ever repay you?"

"You have done already", said the nightingale. "The first time I sang I brought tears to your eyes—I shall never forget that. Those are the jewels that rejoice a singer's heart ... But sleep now and get well and strong again! I will sing to you."

And the nightingale sang, and the Emperor fell into a sweet sleep—such a peaceful, refreshing sleep. When he awoke, restored once more to health, the sun was shining in through the windows. None of his servants

265

had come back yet, for they thought he was dead; but the nightingale was still singing outside.

"You must never leave me again", said the Emperor. "You shall only sing when you want to, and the artificial bird—I shall break it into a thousand pieces."

"No, don't do that," said the nightingale. "It's done what it could; don't part with it yet. I can't make my home in the palace, but let me come when I feel that I want to; then I'll sit of an evening on this branch by the window, and my singing can make you both gay and thoughtful. I shall sing of those that are happy, and of those that suffer; I shall sing of the good and the evil that are here lurking about you. Your little songbird must fly round to distant homes—to the poor fisherman and the humble peasant—to those who are far from you and your Court. I love your heart better than your crown ... and yet there's a breath of something holy about the crown ... I shall come, I shall sing to you; yet there's one thing you must promise me."

"Whatever you ask!" answered the Emperor, standing there in the imperial robes that he had himself put on and holding the heavy gold sword to his heart.

"One thing only I ask of you. Let no one know that you have a little bird who tells you everything; that will be best." And then the nightingale flew away.

The servants came in to look after their dead Emperor. Yes, there they stood, and the Emperor said, "Good morning!"

THE TOP AND THE BALL

A top and a ball were in a drawer together with some other toys, and then one day the top said to the ball: "Look here, we live together in the same drawer—shall we become engaged?" But the ball, who was made of morocco leather and fancied herself quite as much as any smart young lady, wouldn't even answer such a ridiculous question.

Next day the little boy whom the toys belonged to came and painted the top red and yellow all over and hammered a brass nail into the middle of it. The top was really a fine sight, as it went spinning round and round.

"Look at me!" said the top to the ball. "What do you say now? Don't you think after all we might be engaged? We go so splendidly together: you bounce and I dance. There couldn't be a happier couple than us two."

"Oh, you think that, do you?" answered the ball. You don't seem to realise that my father and mother were morocco slippers and that I have a cork inside me."

"Ah, but I'm made of mahogany," said the top. "Why, the mayor turned me himself on his own lathe, and he was so pleased about it."

"Am I really expected to believe that?" asked the ball.

"May I never be whipped again, if I'm not telling you the truth!" answered the top.

"You give a very fine account of yourself," said the ball. "But I really must say no. You see, I'm what you might call half-engaged to a swallow. Every time I go up in the air, he pops his head out of the nest and says: 'Will you? Will you? I've already said to myself that I will, and that's as good as a half-engagement. But I promise never to forget you."

"A lot of good that'll be!" replied the top; and they said no more to each other.

Next day the ball was taken out into the garden. The top watched how she flew high up into the air, just like a bird, until she went clean out of sight. But she came back again each time and, whether from longing or because she had a cork inside her, this was always followed by a high bounce as soon as she touched the ground. The ninth time the ball went up, she never came back; the little boy looked and looked, but she had vanished.

"Ah, I could tell him where she is," said the top with a sigh. "She's in the swallow's nest and has married the swallow."

The more the top thought it all over, the more he lost his heart to the ball. The mere fact that he couldn't have her made him love her more than ever; the strange thing was that she should have accepted anyone else.

And the top went on dancing and spinning round, but all the time he was thinking about the ball, who grew more and more beautiful in his imagination. In this way several years went by, till gradually it became nothing more than an old love-affair ...

But, although the top was no longer young, suddenly one day he found himself painted all over with gold. Never had he looked so handsome; he was now a gold top, and he whirled and whirled until he hummed. Gosh! It was something like! Then all at once he jumped too high—and disappeared. They looked and looked, even down in the basement, but he was not to be found.

Wherever had he got to?

He had jumped into the dustbin among all sorts of cabbage-stalks, sweepings and rubbish that had come down from the gutter on the roof.

"Here's a nice place for me to come to!" said the top. My gold paint will soon go off and—did you ever see such riff-raff as I've got around me!" And then he peeped sideways at a long skinny-looking cabbage-stalk

271

and a curious round object that looked like
an old apple ... But it wasn't an apple at
all, it was an old ball that had been lying
up in the gutter on the roof for several years
and become quite sodden.

"Thank goodness, here's someone at last of
one's own class that one can talk to," said
the ball, with a glance at the gilded top.
"Actually I'm made of morocco leather,
stitched by gentlewomen, and I've got a cork
inside me, but nobody would ever think so
to look at me. I was just going to marry a
swallow, when I landed up in the gutter;
and there I've been for five years growing
more and more sodden. That's a long time,
believe me, for a young lady."

But the top didn't say a word. His thoughts
went back to his old sweetheart, and the
longer he listened the more certain he became that this was her.

Presently the maidservant came to clear
out the dustbin. "Well, I never! Here's the
gold top!" she said. Back in the house the
top came in for lots of attention, but nothing
was said about the ball, and the top never

272

spoke again of his old love. Love is, of course, bound to fade away, when your sweetheart has spent five years growing sodden in a gutter; you can't be expected to know her again, if you meet her in a dustbin.

THE UGLY DUCKLING

Summer-time! How lovely it was out in the country, with the wheat standing yellow, the oats green, and the hay all stacked down in the grassy meadows! And there went the stork on his long red legs, chattering away in Egyptian, for he had learnt that language from his mother. The fields and meadows had large woods all around, and in the middle of the woods there were deep lakes.

Yes, it certainly was lovely out in the country. Bathed in sunshine stood an old manor-house with a deep moat round it, and growing out of the wall down by the water were huge dock-leaves; the biggest of them were so tall that little children could stand upright underneath. The place was as tangled and twisty as the densest forest, and here it was that a duck was sitting on her nest. It was time for her to hatch out her little ducklings, but it was such a long job that she was beginning to lose patience. She hardly ever had a visitor; the other ducks thought more of swimming about in the moat than of coming and sitting under a dock-leaf just for the sake of a quack with her.

At last the eggs cracked open one after the other—"peep! peep!"—and all the yolks had come to life and were sticking out their heads.

"Quack, quack!" said the mother duck, and then the little ones scuttled out as quickly as they could, prying all round under the green leaves; and she let them do this as much as they liked, because green is so good for the eyes.

"Oh, how big the world is!" said the ducklings. And they certainly had much more room now than when they were lying in the egg.

"Do you suppose this is the whole world?" said their mother. "Why, it goes a long way past the other side of the garden, right into the parson's field; but I've never been as far as that. Well, you're all out now, I hope"—and she got up from her nest— "no, not all; the largest egg is still here. How ever long will it be? I can't bother about it much more." And she went on sitting again.

"Well, how's it going?" asked an old duck who came to pay a call.

"There's just this one egg that's taking such a time," said the sitting duck. "It simply won't break. But just look at the others—the loveliest ducklings I've ever seen. They all take after their father—the wretch! Why doesn't he come and see me?"

"Let's have a look at the egg which won't

crack," said the old duck. "I'll bet it's a turkey's egg. That's how I was bamboozled once. The little ones gave me no end of trouble, for they were afraid of the water —fancy that!—I just couldn't get them to go in. I quacked and clacked, but it was no good. Let's have a look at the egg ... Ay, that's a turkey's egg, depend upon it! Let it be, and teach the others to swim."

"I think I'll sit just a little while yet," said the duck. "I've been sitting so long that it won't hurt to sit a little longer."

"Please yourself!" said the old duck, and away she waddled.

At last the big egg cracked. There was a "peep! peep!" from the young one as he tumbled out, looking so large and ugly. The duck glanced at him and said: "My! what a huge great duckling that is! None of the others look a bit like that. Still, it's never a turkey-chick, I'll be bound ... Well, we shall soon find out. He shall go into the water, if I have to kick him in myself!"

The next day the weather was gloriously fine, with sun shining on all the green dock-leaves. The mother duck with her whole family came down to the moat. Splash! into the water she jumped. "Quack, quack!" she said, and one after another the ducklings plomped in after her. The water closed over their heads, but they were up again in a moment and floated along so beautifully. Their legs worked of their own accord, and now the whole lot were in the water—even the ugly grey duckling joined in the swimming.

"It's no turkey, that's certain," said the duck. "Look how beautifully he uses his legs and how straight he holds himself. He's my own little one all right, and he's quite handsome, when you really come to look at him. Quack, quack! Now, come along with me and let me show you the world and introduce you all to the barnyard, but mind and keep close to me, so that nobody steps on you; and keep a sharp look-out for the cat."

Then they made their way into the duck-yard. There was a fearful noise going on, for there were two families fighting for an eel's head, and after all it was the cat that got it.

"You see! That's the way of the world," said the mother duck and licked her bill, for she too had fancied the eel's head. "Now then, where are your legs?" she said. "Look slippy and make a nice bow to the old duck over there. She's the most genteel of all these; she has Spanish blood, that's why she's so plump. And do you see that crimson rag she wears on one leg? It's extremely fine; it's the highest distinction any duck can win. It's as good as saying that there is no thought of getting rid of her; man and beast are to take notice! Look alive, and don't turn your toes in! A well-bred duckling turns its toes out, like father and mother ... That's it. Now make a bow and say 'quack!' "

They all obeyed; but the other ducks round about looked at them and said out loud: "There! Now we've got to have that rabble as well—as if there weren't enough of us already! Ugh! What a sight that duckling is! We can't possibly put up with him" —and one duck immediately flew at him and bit him in the neck.

"Leave him alone," said the mother. "He's doing no one any harm."

"Yes, but he's so gawky and peculiar," said the one that had pecked him, "so he'll have to be squashed."

"What pretty children you have, my dear!" said the old duck with the rag on her leg. "All of them but one, who doesn't seem right. I only wish you could make him all over again."

"No question of that, my lady," said the ducklings' mother. "He's not pretty, but he's so good-tempered and he can swim just as well as the others—I daresay even a bit better. I fancy his looks will improve as he grows up, or maybe in time he'll grow down a little. He lay too long in the egg—that's why he isn't quite the right shape." And then she plucked his neck for him and smoothed out his feathers. "Anyhow, he's a drake, and so it doesn't matter so much," she added. "I feel sure he'll turn out pretty strong and be able to manage all right."

"The other ducklings are charming," said the old duck. "Make yourselves at home, my dears, and if you should find such a thing as an eel's head, you may bring it to me."

And so they made themselves at home.

But the poor duckling who was the last out of the egg and looked so ugly got pecked and jostled and teased by ducks and hens alike. "The great gawk!" they all clucked. And the turkey, who was born with spurs and therefore thought himself an emperor, puffed up his feathers like a ship under full sail and went straight at him, and then he gobble-gobbled till he was quite red in the face. The poor duckling didn't know where to turn; he was terribly upset over being so ugly and the laughing-stock of the whole barnyard.

That's how it was the first day, and afterwards things grew worse and worse. The poor duckling got chivied about by all of them; even his own brothers and sisters treated him badly, and they kept saying: "If only the cat would get you, you ridiculous great guy!" And the mother herself wished he were far away. The ducks nipped him, the hens pecked him, and the maid who had to feed the poultry let fly at him with her foot.

After that, he ran away and fluttered over the hedge, and the little birds in the bushes grew frightened and flew into the air. "That's because I'm so ugly," thought the duckling and closed his eyes—and yet managed to get away. Eventually he came out to the great marsh where the wild-ducks lived and lay there all night, utterly tired and dispirited.

In the morning the wild-ducks flew up and looked at their new companion. "What ever are you?" they asked, and the duckling turned in every direction and bowed as well as he could.

"What a scarecrow you are!" said the wild-ducks, "but that won't matter to us, as long as you don't marry into our family." Poor thing! He wasn't dreaming of getting married; all he wanted was to be allowed to stay quietly among the rushes and drink a little marsh-water. After he had been there for two whole days, two wild-geese came along—or rather two wild-ganders, for they were both males. It was not long since they were hatched; that's why they were so perky.

"Look here, my lad!" they began. "You are so ugly that quite like you. Will you come in with us and migrate? Not far off, in another marsh, are some very nice young wild-geese, none of them married, who can quack beautifully. Here's a chance for you to make a hit, ugly as you are."

"Bang! bang!" suddenly echoed above them, and both the ganders fell down dead in the rushes, and the water became red with blood. "Bang! bang!" sounded once more, and flocks of wild-geese flew up from the rushes, so that immediately fresh shots rang out. A big shoot was on. The party lay ready all round the marsh; some even sat up in the trees on the branches that stretched right out over the rushes. Clouds of blue smoke drifted in among the dark trees and hung far over the water. Splashing through the mud came the gun-dogs, bending back reeds and rushes this way and that. It was terrifying for the poor duckling, who was just turning his head round to bury it under his wing when he suddenly found close beside him a fearsome great dog with lolling tongue and grim, glittering eyes. It lowered its muzzle right down to the duckling, bared its sharp teeth and—splash! it went off again without touching him.

The duckling gave a sigh of relief. "Thank goodness, I'm so ugly that even the dog doesn't fancy the taste of me." And he lay there quite still, while the shot pattered on the reeds and crack after crack was heard from the guns.

It was late in the day before everything was quiet again, but the poor duckling didn't dare to get up yet; he waited several hours longer before he took a look round and then made off from the marsh as fast as he could go. Over field and meadow he scuttled, but there was such a wind that he found it difficult to get along.

Towards evening he came up to a poor little farm-cottage; it was so broken-down that it hardly knew which way to fall, and so it remained standing. The wind whizzed so fiercely round the duckling that he had to sit on his tail so as not to be blown over. The wind grew worse and worse. Then he noticed that the door had come off one of its hinges and hung so much on the slant that he could slip into the house through the crack. And that's just what he did.

There was an old woman living here with her cat and her hen. The cat, whom she called Sonny, could arch its back and purr; it could even give out sparks, if you stroked its fur the wrong way. The hen had such short little legs that it was called Chicka-biddy Shortlegs; it was a very good layer, and the woman loved it like her own child.

Next morning they at once noticed the strange duckling, and the cat started to purr and the hen to cluck. "Why, what's up?" said the woman, looking round. But her sight wasn't very good, and she took the duckling for a fat duck that had lost its way. "My! What a find!" she said. "I shall be able to have duck's eggs—as long it isn't a drake! We must give it a trial."

And so the duckling was taken on trial for three weeks; but there was no sign of an egg.

Now, the cat was master in the house and the hen was mistress, and they always used to say "We and the world," because they fancied that they made up half the world—

what's more, much the superior half of it. The duckling thought there might be two opinions about that, but the hen wouldn't hear of it.

"Can you lay eggs?" she asked.

"No."

"Well, then, hold your tongue, will you!"

And the cat asked: "Can you arch your back or purr or give out sparks?"

"No."

"Well, then, your opinion's not wanted, when sensible people are talking."

And the duckling sat in the corner, quite out of spirits. Then suddenly he remembered the fresh air and the sunshine, and he got such a curious longing to swim in the water that—he couldn't help it—he had to tell the hen.

"What's the matter with you?" she asked. "You haven't anything to do—that's why you get these fancies. They'd soon go, if only you'd lay eggs or else purr."

"But it's so lovely to swim in the water," said the duckling; "so lovely to duck your head in it and dive down to the bottom."

"Most enjoyable, I'm sure," said the hen. "You must have gone crazy. Ask the cat about it—I've never met any one as clever as he is—ask him if he's fond of swimming or diving! I say nothing of myself. Ask our old mistress, the wisest woman in the world! Do you suppose that she's keen on swimming and diving?"

"You don't understand me," said the duckling.

"Well, if we don't understand you, I should like to know who would. Surely you'll never try and make out you are wiser than the cat and the mistress—not to mention myself. Don't be silly, child! Give thanks to your Maker for all the kindness you have met with. Haven't you come to a nice warm room, where you have company that can teach you something? But you're just a stupid, and there's no fun in having you here. You may take my word for it—if I say unpleasant things to you, it's all for your good; that's just how you can tell which are your real friends. Only see that you lay eggs and learn how to purr or give out sparks!"

288

"I think I'll go out into the wide world,"
said the duckling.

"Yes, do," said the hen.

And so the duckling went off. He swam in
the water; he dived down; but none of them
would nave anything to do with him because
of his ugliness.

Autumn now set in. The leaves in the
wood turned yellow and brown, the wind
seized them and whirled them about, while
the sky above had a frosty look. The clouds
hung heavy with hail and snow, and the
raven who perched on the fence kept
squawking "ow! ow!"—he felt so cold.
The very thought of it gave you the shivers.
Yes, the poor duckling was certainly having
a bad time.

One evening, when there was a lovely
sunset, a whole flock of large handsome
birds appeared out of the bushes. The
duckling had never seen such beautiful birds,
all glittering white with long graceful necks.
They were swans. They gave the most
extraordinary cry, spread out their magnificent long wings and flew from this cold

country away to warmer lands and open lakes.

They mounted high, high up into the air, and the ugly little duckling felt so strange as he watched them. He turned round and round in the water like a wheel and craned his neck in their direction, letting out a cry so shrill and strange that it quite scared even himself. Ah! he could never forget those beautiful, fortunate birds; and directly they were lost to sight he dived right down to the bottom and, when he came up again, he was almost beside himself. He had no idea what the birds were called, nor where they were flying to, and yet they were dearer to him than any he had ever known; he didn't envy them in the least—how could he ever dream of such loveliness for himself? He would be quite satisfied, if only the ducks would just put up with him, poor gawky-looking creature!

What a cold winter it was! The duckling had to keep swimming about in the water to prevent it freezing right up. But every night the pool he was swimming in grew smaller and smaller; then the ice froze so hard that you could hear it creaking. The duckling had to keep his feet moving all the time to prevent the water from closing up. At last he grew faint with exhaustion and lay quite still and finally froze fast in the ice.

Early next morning he was seen by a peasant who went out and broke the ice with his wooden clog and carried the duckling home to his wife. And there they revived him.

The children wanted to play with him, but the duckling was afraid they meant mischief and fluttered in panic right up into the milk-bowl, so that the milk slopped over into the room. The woman screamed out and clapped her hands in the air, and then he flew into the butter-tub, and from there down into the flour-bin, and out of it again. Dear, dear, he did look an object! The woman screamed at him and hit at him with the tongs, and the children tumbled over each other trying to catch him—how they laughed and shouted! ... It was a good thing the door was open; the duckling darted out into the bushes and sank down, dazed, in the new-fallen snow.

But it would be far too dismal to describe all the want and misery the duckling had to go through during that hard winter ... He was sheltering among the reeds on the marsh, when the sun began to get warm again and the larks to sing; beautiful spring had arrived.

Then all at once he tried his wings; the whirr of them was louder than before, and they carried him swiftly away. Almost before he realised it, he found himself in a big garden with apple-trees in blossom and sweet-smelling lilac that dangled from long green boughs right over the winding stream. Oh, it was so lovely here in all the freshness of spring! And straight ahead, out of the thicket, came three beautiful white swans, ruffling their feathers and floating so lightly on the water. The duckling recognised the splendid creatures and was overcome with a strange feeling of melancholy.

"I will fly across to them, those royal birds! They will peck me to death for daring, ugly as I am, to go near them. Never mind! Better to be killed by them than be nipped by the ducks, pecked by the hens, kicked by the girl who minds the poultry, and suffer hardship in winter." And he flew out on to the water and swam towards the beautiful swans. As they caught sight of him, they darted with ruffled feathers to meet him. "Yes, kill me, kill me!" cried the poor creature and bowed his head to the water awaiting death. But what did he see there in the clear stream? It was a reflection of himself that he saw in front of him, but no longer a clumsy greyish bird, ugly and unattractive —no, he was himself a swan!

It doesn't matter about being born in a duckyard, as long as you are hatched from a swan's egg.

He felt positively glad at having gone through so much hardship and want; it helped him to appreciate all the happiness and beauty that were there to welcome him ... And the three great swans swam round and round and stroked him with their beaks.

Some little children came into the garden

and threw bread and grain into the water,
and the smallest one called out: "There's a
new swan!" and the other children joined
in with shouts of delight: "Yes, there's a new
swan!" And they clapped their hands and
danced about and ran to fetch father and
mother. Bits of bread and cake were thrown
into the water, and everyone said: "The new
one is the prettiest—so young and handsome!" And the old swans bowed before
him.

This made him feel quite shy, and he
tucked his head away under his wing—he
himself hardly knew why. He was too, too
happy, but not a bit proud, for a good heart

is never proud. He thought of how he had been despised and persecuted, and now he heard everybody saying that he was the loveliest of all lovely birds. And the lilacs bowed their branches to him right down to the water, and the sunshine felt so warm and kindly. Then he ruffled his feathers, raised his slender neck and rejoiced from his heart: "I never dreamed of so much happiness, when I was the ugly duckling."

THE SNOW QUEEN
A story in seven parts.

1

The looking-glass and the broken bits

Now look out! We're going to begin. When we've come to the end of this part, we shall know more than we do now; for it has to do with a wicked imp—one of the very wickedest—Old Nick. One day he was in excellent spirits, because he had made a looking-glass which had this about it—that everything good and beautiful that was reflected in it shrank up into almost nothing, whereas everything useless and ugly stood out worse than ever. In this glass the loveliest scenery looked like boiled spinach, and even the nicest people became nasty or stood on their heads and had no stomachs. Faces were so twisted that you couldn't recognize them, and if you happened to have one freckle you could be sure that it would spread all over nose and mouth. That was huge fun, according to Old Nick. Suppose a person had some kind, good thought, a horrible leer was reflected in the looking-glass, which made Nick roar with laughter at his clever invention. Everyone who went to the imp-school—for he kept a school for imps —went about saying there had been a miracle: now for the first time (they declared) one could see what people and things really looked like. They ran about all over the place with the looking-glass, till at last there wasn't a country or a person that hadn't been changed for the worse in this way.

And now they decided to fly up to heaven

and make fun of the angels and of God Himself. The higher they flew with the looking-glass, the more horribly it leered—they could scarcely hold on to it. Up and up they went, nearer and nearer to God and the angels. All at once the glass quivered so terribly from its grimace that it flew out of their hands and went crashing down to earth, where it burst into a hundred million billion pieces, and even more than that; in fact, it now did much worse damage than before. You see, some pieces were hardly bigger than a grain of sand; and these flew round the whole wide world, and whenever they got into people's eyes they stuck there, and a person saw everything wrong or only saw the worst side of a thing, for every little glass-splinter had kept the same powers as the whole looking-glass. Some people even got a little bit of glass in their hearts, and that was too terrible; the heart became just like a lump of ice. A few fragments were so big that they got used as window-panes, but it was better not to see your friends through windows of that sort. Other pieces were fitted into spectacles and, when people put on their glasses in order to see properly and fairly, then things didn't go at all well; and the devil laughed till he split—he was simply tickled to death.

But outside there were still little bits of glass whirling about in the air. Just listen to what happened.

2

A little boy and a little girl

In the great city—where there are so many houses and people that there isn't room for everyone to have a little garden of his own, so most of them have to be content with flowers in flower-pots—there lived two poor children who *did* have a garden a bit larger than a flower-pot. They weren't brother and sister, but they were just as fond of each other as if they had been. Their parents were next-door neighbours, living in attics; at the point where their roofs were almost touching and the gutter ran along between the eaves, each house had a window facing the other. You only had to step over the gutter to cross from window to window.

The parents of the two children each had a big wooden box outside, and in this grew pot-herbs, which they used, and a little rose tree; there was one in each box, and they grew beautifully. Then the parents thought of placing the boxes across the gutter in such a way that they nearly reached from one window to the other and looked exactly like two banks of flowers. The sweet-pea tendrils hung down over the boxes; the rose-trees put out long branches, twining round the windows and leaning toward each other; it was almost a triumphal arch of greenery and flowers. As the boxes were very high and the two children knew that they mustn't crawl up on to them, they often got leave to climb out to each other and, sitting on their

301

little stools under the roses, had wonderful games there together.

In winter, of course, that sort of fun came to an end. The window-panes were often frosted right over; but then they warmed up pennies on the stove, placed the heated coin on the frozen pane, and in this way made a splendid peep-hole, as round as could be. Behind, there peeped a gentle, loving eye, one from each window. It was the little boy and the little girl; his name was Kay, hers was Gerda. In summer they could reach each other with a single jump; in winter they must first go down a lot of stairs, then up a lot of stairs, while outside the snow would be steadily falling.

"Those are the white bees swarming," said the old grandmother.

"Have they got a queen as well?" asked the little boy, for he knew that the real bees have a sort of queen.

"Yes, they have," said the grandmother. "She flies just where the swarm is thickest, and she's the biggest of them all. She never lies still on the ground; she flies up again into the black cloud. On many a winter night she flies through the streets of the town and peeps in at the windows, and then they freeze into curious patterns, just like flowers."

"Yes, I've seen that!" cried both children at once, and so they knew it was true.

"Can the Snow Queen come in here?" asked the little girl.

"Just let her have a go," said the boy; "I'll put her on the hot stove, and she'll melt."

But the grandmother smoothed his hair and told them some other stories.

In the evening, when little Kay was home again and half-undressed, he crawled up on to the chairs by the window and peeped out through the little hole. A few snowflakes were falling outside, and one of these, the biggest of them all, remained lying on the edge of one of the flower-boxes. The snow-flake grew larger and larger, till at last it became the figure of a woman dressed in the most delicate white gauze, which was made up of millions of tiny star-shaped flakes. She

303

was pretty and distinguished-looking, but a figure of ice, glaring glittering ice. Yet she was alive; her eyes stared like two bright stars, but there was no peace or quiet in them. She nodded towards the window and beckoned with her hand. The little boy grew frightened and jumped down from the chair; and at that moment a large bird seemed to fly past the window.

Next day there was a clear frost, and this was followed by a thaw; after that came the spring. The sun shone, bits of green peeped out, the swallows built their nests, the windows were thrown open, and once more the two little children sat in their little garden high up by the gutter at the very top of the house.

The roses were especially fine that summer. The little girl had learnt a hymn that had a bit about roses in it, and these roses made her think of her own. She sang it to the little boy, and he joined in:

"The valley glows with many a rose,
    and there we meet the Sacred Child."

And the two children took each other's

hands and kissed the roses; they looked up at God's bright sunshine and spoke to it as if the Holy Child were there. What beautiful summer days those were! How wonderful it was to be out beside the fresh rose-trees, which never seemed to want to stop blooming!

Kay and Gerda sat looking at the picture-book of birds and animals, when suddenly, just as five o'clock was striking from the tall church-tower, Kay called out, "Ow! something's pricked me in the heart. Ow! and now I've got something in my eye."

The little girl put her arm round his neck; he blinked his eyes. No, there was nothing to be seen.

"I expect it's gone," he said. But it hadn't gone. It just happened to be one of those glass splinters that flew from the looking-glass—the imp glass—you remember, don't you, that horrid glass which made everything great and good that was reflected in it seem small and ugly, while what was evil and wicked stood out sharply and every flaw showed up at once. Sure enough, poor

Kay had received a piece right in his heart, which would presently turn into a lump of ice. For the moment the piece of glass had stopped hurting, but it was still there.

"Gerda, why are you crying?" he asked. "It makes you look so ugly. There's nothing whatever the matter with me. Ugh!" he cried suddenly, "that rose has got a worm in it, and look how crooked that one's growing. They're rotten roses, when you come to think of it—just like the boxes they're growing in." And he kicked the box hard and broke off the two roses.

"Kay, what are you doing?" exclaimed the little girl; and when he saw how upset she was, he broke off another rose and ran in at his window away from dear little Gerda.

Next time she got out the picture-book, he said the book was babyish; and if their grandmother told them stories, he always chipped in with an "Ah, but—." He would even, if he got the chance, go behind her, put on some spectacles and talk just like her. It was a perfect imitation and made people laugh. After a while he could mimic the voice and the walk of every single person in the street. Kay knew how to take off all their awkward peculiarities, so that people said, "That boy certainly has a remarkable head on him." But no, it was the bit of glass in his eye, the bit of glass in his heart, that made him tease even little Gerda, who loved him from the bottom of her heart.

The games he played now were quite different to the old ones; they were quite brainy. One winter's day, as the snowflakes were drifting down, he picked up a big burning-glass and, holding out the flap of his blue coat, he let the snowflakes fall on it.

"Take a peep through this glass, Gerda," he said; and every snowflake became much larger and looked like a splendid flower or a ten-pointed star. It was a wonderful sight.

"Do you see how cunning that is?" said Kay. "These are much more interesting than real flowers. And there isn't a single flaw in them; they are perfect in every way, as long as they don't melt."

A little later Kay arrived with big gloves on and his toboggan on his back. He shouted into Gerda's ears that he had been told he might go tobogganing in the main Square where the others were playing, and away he went.

Over in the Square the boldest boys often tied their toboggans on to the farmer's cart and in that way went with it a good distance. It was grand sport. In the midst of the fun a large sledge drove up, all painted dead white. In it sat a figure, muffled in a white fur coat and wearing a white fur cap. The sledge drove twice round the Square, and in a twinkling Kay managed to fasten his toboggan behind it, so that it pulled him along. Faster and faster they went, straight into the next street. The driver of the sledge, with a turn of the head, gave Kay a friendly nod just as though they knew each other; and each time that Kay thought of loosening his little toboggan, the person nodded again, and so Kay stayed where he was, and they drove straight out of the town-gate. Now the snow began to fall so thickly that the boy couldn't see his hand in front of his face as he rushed along. He quickly let loose the rope, so as to get away from the big sledge. But that was no use; his little toboggan still clung to it, and they scudded along like the wind. He yelled at the top of his voice, but no one heard him; and the snow whirled down, and the sledge flew on. Now and then it did a jump, as though they were crossing ditches and hedges. Kay was absolutely terrified; he tried to say the Lord's Prayer, but all he could remember was the multiplication table.

The snowflakes got bigger and bigger, till at last they looked like great white chickens. All at once they sprang aside, the big sledge stopped, and the driver stood up. Coat and cap were pure snow; it was a woman, tall and straight, white and glittering. It was the Snow Queen.

"We've covered the ground well," she said. "But do you feel cold? Creep into my bearskin." And she put him beside her in the sledge and wrapped the furs round him; it was like sinking into a snowdrift.

"Are you still cold?" she asked, and then she kissed his forehead. Uh! Her kiss was

309

colder than ice, it went right to his heart, which was anyhow nearly a lump of ice already. He felt as if he were dying—but only for a moment. After that all was well, and he didn't notice the cold any more.

"My sledge! Don't forget my little sledge!" That was the first thing he thought of, and it was fastened to one of the white chickens, which came flying along behind them with the toboggan on its back. The Snow Queen kissed Kay once more, and after that he had quite forgotten little Gerda and Grannie and all the others at home.

"You mustn't have any more kisses," said the Snow Queen, "or else I shall kiss you to death."

Kay looked at her. She was very beautiful; he couldn't imagine a more intelligent, lovelier face. She no longer seemed to be just a figure of ice, as she did that time she sat outside the window and beckoned to him. In his eyes she was perfect. He didn't feel a bit afraid, but described to her how he could do mental arithmetic, even with fractions, and that he knew the number of square miles there were to the different countries and "what's the population?" And she kept smiling back at him, so that he began to think that perhaps what he knew was hardly enough. And he looked up into the great spaces of the sky, and she flew along with him, high up on the black cloud; and the wind roared and whistled—it reminded one of the old folksongs. They flew over woods and lakes, over sea and land; below them the icy blast whistled, the wolves howled, the snow sparkled as the black crows flew screaming across it; but high above everything shone the great silver moon. Kay gazed up at it through the long, long winter night; by day he slept at the Snow Queen's feet.

3

The flower garden of the old woman who could do magic

But how was little Gerda getting on, when Kay didn't come back? Wherever had he got to? No one knew, no one could give any news of him. The boys simply described how they had seen him tie his toboggan to a fine great sledge which drove down the street and out by the town-gate. Nobody knew where he was. There was great grief, and little Gerda cried her heart out. Then people said that he was dead, that he had fallen into the river which ran close to the town. What a long, gloomy winter it was!

And now the spring arrived with warmer sunshine.

"Kay's dead and gone," said little Gerda.

"I don't believe it," said the sunshine.

"He's dead and gone," she said to the swallows.

"I don't believe it," was the answer; and in the end little Gerda didn't believe it either.

"I'll put on my new red shoes," she said one morning. "The ones Kay has never seen, and then I'll go down to the river and question it."

It was early morning when she kissed her sleeping Grannie, put on the red shoes and walked all by herself out of the town-gate down to the river.

"Is it true that you've taken my little playmate? I'll give you my red shoes, if you'll give him back to me."

And the waves seemed to nod back at her curiously. Then she took off her red shoes, the dearest possession she had, and threw them both out into the river; but they fell close in to the bank, and the little waves

313

brought them straight back to her. It was just as though the river didn't like to rob her of her dearest possession, because it hadn't anyhow taken little Kay. But now Gerda felt that perhaps she hadn't thrown the shoes far enough out; so she climbed into a boat that lay among the rushes and went right along to the far end of it and threw the shoes overboard. But the boat had not been made fast and, at the movement she gave it, it drifted from the bank. She noticed this and made haste to escape, but before she could get back the boat was a couple of yards from the shore, and now it gathered speed as it glided away.

At this Gerda grew very frightened and began to cry, but nobody heard her except the sparrows, and they couldn't carry her ashore, but they flew along the bank, as if to comfort her with their chirping, „Here we are, here we are!" The boat drifted with the stream, while little Gerda sat quite still in her stocking-feet. Her red shoes were floating behind, but they couldn't catch the boat, which had more way on.

It was very pretty on both banks: old

trees, lovely flowers, and grassy slopes with sheep and cows, but not a person in sight.

"Perhaps the river will carry me to little Kay," thought Gerda, and that raised her spirits. She stood up and gazed for hours at the delightful green banks. Eventually she came to a large cherry-orchard, where there was a little house with curious red and blue windows, also a thatched roof and two wooden soldiers outside presenting arms to all who sailed past.

Gerda called out to them, thinking they were alive, but of course they didn't answer. She came quite close to them, as the river drove the boat straight into the bank.

Gerda called out still louder, and that brought out of the house an old, old woman leaning on a crutch-handled stick; she was wearing a large sun-hat, which was painted over with most beautiful flowers.

"You poor child!" said the old woman. "How ever did you come to be driven on to this great rolling river, far out into the wide world?" Then the old woman went right into the water and, hooking the boat with her stick, drew it in to the bank and lifted little Gerda out. Gerda was glad to be on dry land again, though a little bit frightened of the strange old woman. "Now come and tell me who you are and how you come to be here," she said.

Then Gerda told her everything, and the old woman shook her head and said, "dear me!" And when Gerda had finished her story and asked if she had seen little Kay, the woman said that he hadn't come past there; but he might, though, and Gerda mustn't be downhearted but taste some of her cherries and have a look at her flowers, which were prettier than any picture-book and could each of them tell a complete story. Then she took Gerda by the hand, and they went inside the little house, and the old woman shut the door behind her.

The windows were high up on the walls, with red, blue and yellow glass in them. The daylight shone strangely into the room with all these colours, but on the table was a plate of the finest cherries, and Gerda was allowed to eat as many of them as she liked.

316

While she was eating, the old woman combed her hair with a gold comb, and her bright yellow curls made a charming frame for the kind little face, which was so round and rosy.

"I've always longed for a nice little girl like you," said the woman. "Just you see how well we shall get on together, you and I;" and as she combed little Gerda's hair, Gerda forgot her foster-brother Kay more and more. You see, the old woman could do magic, but she wasn't a wicked magician; she only did a little magic for her own enjoyment, and at present she very much wanted to keep little Gerda. So she went out into the garden, reached out her stick to all the rose-trees and, however beautifully they were in bloom, they all sank down into the black earth leaving no sign of where they had stood. The old woman was afraid that, if Gerda saw the roses, she might think of the ones they had at home and then remember little Kay and run off.

Now she took Gerda out into the flower-garden. Goodness, what fragrance and beauty there was! Every flower you could think of, at whatever season of the year, stood here in full bloom; no picture-book could be more gay and attractive. Gerda jumped for joy and played about until the sun went down behind the tall cherry-trees. Then she was given a charming bed with red silk pillows that were stuffed with blue violets, and there she slept and dreamt as wonderfully as any queen on her wedding-day.

The next morning she was again able to play with the flowers in the sunshine, and in this way a number of days went by. Gerda knew every flower, but however many there were she somehow felt there was one missing, though she didn't know which. And then one day she was sitting looking at the old woman's sun-hat with the flowers painted on it and, sure enough, the prettiest of them all was a rose. The woman had forgotten to remove it from her hat that time she made the other roses sink down into the ground. That comes of not having your wits about you! "What!" said Gerda, "no roses in the garden!" And she ran in and out of the flower-beds and looked and looked, but there wasn't a rose to be found. Then she sat down and cried; but her hot tears fell just where a rose-tree had sunk and, as their warmth watered the ground, the tree suddenly sprouted up, just as blooming as when it sank; and Gerda embraced it and kissed the roses, while her thoughts turned to the lovely roses at home and so to little Kay.

"Oh, how I've been delayed!" said the little girl. "I was to go and find Kay! Do you know where he is?" she asked the roses. "Do you think he's dead and gone?"

"No, he's not dead," said the roses. "You see, we've been in the earth ourselves; that's where all the dead are, but Kay wasn't there."

"Thank you," said little Gerda, and she went off to the other flowers and looked into their cups and asked, "Do you know where Kay is?"

But every flower was standing in the sun and dreaming its own fairy-tale or romance. Gerda was told ever so many of those, but nobody knew anything about Kay.

And what did the tiger-lily say?

319

"Listen to the drum—boom, boom! There are only two notes—boom, boom! Hark to the women's dirge! Hark to the cry of the priests! The Hindoo woman stands on the funeral pyre in her long red robe, the flames fly up around her and her dead husband; but the Hindoo woman is thinking of the living man there in the crowd, whose eyes burn hotter than the flames, whose fiery glances come nearer to her heart than the flames that will soon burn her body to ashes. Can the heart's flame perish in the flames of the pyre?"

"I can't understand what that's all about," said little Gerda. "That's my story," said the tiger-lily.

What does the convolvulus say?

"Overhanging the narrow mountain-road stands an ancient castle. Creepers grow thick about the old red walls, climbing leaf by leaf right over the balcony. And there stands a graceful girl, leaning over the parapet and looking down the road; no rose hangs fresher on its spray, no apple-blossom that is borne by the breeze

320

from its tree, hovers more lightly. Listen to the frou-frou of her splendid silk dress! 'Is he never coming?'"

"Is that Kay you mean?" asked Gerda.

"I only speak of my own story, my own dream," answered the convolvulus.

What does the little snowdrop say?

"Between the trees is a long board hanging by two ropes; it's a swing. Two pretty little girls in snowy white frocks, with long green ribbons of silk fluttering from their hats, are sitting and swinging. Their brother, who is bigger than they are, is standing up in the swing with his arm round the rope to steady himself, for in one hand he has a little bowl, in the other a clay pipe; he's blowing soap-bubbles. To and fro goes the swing, and the bubbles rise floating in the air with beautiful changing colours; the last one still clings to the pipe, swaying in the wind. The swing rocks on. The little black dog, as lightly as the bubbles, rises on his hind-legs, asking to be taken into the swing. It swoops past, the dog tumbles and yelps angrily, for they're teasing him; the bubbles burst. A swinging board, a picture of leaping froth—that is my song."

"I daresay that's a pretty tale, but you tell it so mournfully, and you don't say anything about Kay. What do the hyacinths say?"

"There were three beautiful sisters, with delicate skin as clear as crystal. One's dress was red, another's blue, and the third one's pure white. Hand in hand they danced beside the calm lake in the silver moonlight. They were not elf-maidens but humans. The air smelt so sweet, and the girls vanished into the wood. The air smelt still sweeter. ... Three coffins, in which lay the beautiful sisters, glided from the heart of the wood away over the lake; fire-flies flew gleaming around like little hovering tapers. Are the dancing maidens asleep or are they dead? The scent of the flowers tells that they are dead; the evening-bell is tolling for the dead."

"You make me quite sad," said little Gerda. "Your scent is so strong; I can't get the dead sisters out of my mind. Oh, but is little Kay really dead? The roses have been down in the earth, and they say no."

"Ding-dong!" tolled the bells of the hyacinth. "We're not tolling for little Kay; we don't know him. We're merely singing our song, the only one we know."

And Gerda went along to the buttercup, shining out among its glistening green leaves. "How brightly you shine, little sun," said Gerda. "Tell me whether you know where I shall find my playmate."

The buttercup shone most beautifully and looked at Gerda once more. What song do you suppose the buttercup could sing? This wasn't about Kay either.

"In a small backyard God's sun was shining warmly on the first day of spring, its beams gliding down the neighbour's white walls. Near by grew the first yellow flowers, glittering like gold in the warm rays of the sun. Old Grannie was out in her chair; her good-looking granddaughter, a humble maidservant, had come home on a short visit, and now she kissed her grandmother. There was gold, gold from the heart, in that blessed kiss. Golden lips, golden power, golden hearts in that morning-hour. There! that's my little story," said the buttercup.

"My poor old Grannie!" sighed Gerda, "She's sure to be longing for me and grieving for me, as she was for little Kay. But I shall soon be home again, and then I shall bring Kay with me ... It's no good my asking the flowers. They only know their own songs; they can tell me nothing." And she tucked up her little frock, so as to be able to run faster. But the narcissus tapped her leg as she jumped over it. She stopped and looked at the tall yellow flower. "Perhaps you have heard something?" she asked. So she stooped right down to the narcissus. And what did she hear?

"I can see myself, I can see myself!" said the narcissus. "Dear, dear! can't you smell me? Up in the little attic-room stands a little dancer. She stands, now on one leg, now on both; her high kicks are for all and sundry. Mere glamour, that's all she is. She pours out water from the teapot on to some garment she's holding; it's her stays —cleanliness is such a good thing! The white frock hanging on the peg, that's also been washed in the teapot and dried on the roof. Now she puts it on, with the saffron-yellow scarf round her neck, so that the frock gleams all the whiter. Up goes her leg! Look at her strutting on one stalk! I can see myself, I can see myself!"

"I don't care a scrap about all that," said Gerda. "It's no story for me!"—and off she ran down to the bottom of the garden.

The gate was locked, but she waggled the rusty latch till it was free; the gate flew open, and little Gerda ran out bare-footed into the wide world. Three times she looked back, but nobody was following her. At last she couldn't run any more but sat down on a big stone; and when she glanced about her, she saw that the summer was over. It was late autumn, but there had been no sign of this in the beautiful garden, where there was always sunshine with flowers belonging to every season of the year.

"My, how I've dawdled!" said little Gerda.

"Why, it's autumn already. I mustn't rest any longer"—and she got up to go.

Oh, how tired and sore her little feet were! The countryside looked cold and damp; the long willow-leaves were quite yellow, shedding misty tears as the leaves dropped one by one. Only the sloe was still bearing fruit, so sharp as to twist your mouth all crooked. Oh, how gloomy and sad the wide world seemed!

4

Prince and Princess

Gerda had to have another rest. Hopping about in the snow, in front of where she sat, was a big crow who had been watching her there for some time and waggling his head. Now he greeted her—"Caw, caw! How do, how do!" That was the best he could manage, but he wanted to help the little girl and asked where she was going, all alone in the wide, wide world. "Alone"—how well Gerda understood that word and what it meant. So then she told the whole story of her life to the crow and asked whether he had seen Kay. The crow nodded thought-

327

fully and said, "Maybe I have, maybe I have."

"Oh, do you think you have?" cried the little girl, nearly squeezing him to death as she kissed him.

"Now then, now then," said the crow. "I quite think it was little Kay. But by this time he will certainly have forgotten you for the Princess."

"Does he live with a princess?" asked Gerda.

"Yes, just listen," said the crow. "But I find it so difficult to talk your language. "Can you understand crow language? I could tell it you better in that."

"No, I've never learnt it," said Gerda, "but Grannie can, and P language, too. I do wish I could."

"Never mind," said the crow. "I'll tell you as best I can, though it won't be up to much, I'm afraid." And then he told her what he knew.

"In the kingdom where we are now lives a Princess who is tremendously clever. You see, she has read all the newspapers there are in the world and forgotten them again. She's as clever as that. The other day she was sitting on the throne—and there's not much fun in that, so I'm told—when she happened to hum a little song that runs like this: 'Why shouldn't I have a husband?' 'Well, there's something to be said for that,' she thought. So she made up her mind to marry, but she wanted a husband who could speak up for himself when spoken to—who didn't just stand and look distinguished, for that's so very dull. Then she rang for all her court ladies and, when they heard what she meant to do, they were delighted. 'How splendid!' they all said. 'That's just what we were thinking the other day.' Believe me," added the crow, "every word I say is true. I've got a tame sweetheart who has a free run of the palace, and she has told me the whole story."

Of course, his sweetheart was also a crow, for birds of a feather flock together.

"The newspapers at once came out with a border of hearts and the Princess's monogram. You could read for yourself that any good-looking young man was free to come up to the palace and talk to the Princess; and the one who spoke so that you felt that he was quite at home there and was the best talker, he was the one the Princess meant to marry. Yes, you can take my word for it," said the crow. "It's as true as I sit here. People came in throngs. There was jostling and hustling but every one of them failed, both on the first day and on the second. They were all good talkers out in the street, but so soon as they came to the palace and saw the guards in silver at the entrance and the lackeys in gold on the stairs and the glitter of the great lighted halls, then they became flurried; and when they stood before the throne where the Princess was sitting, they could do nothing but repeat her last remark, and she had no desire to hear that again. It was just as though people in there had been dosed with snuff which had half sent them to sleep, until they came into the street again; then of course they were perfect chatterboxes. There was a long line of them stretching from the town-gate to the palace. "I saw it all myself," said the crow. "They soon became hungry and thirsty, but from the palace they never received so much as a glass of tepid water. A few of the wiser ones, it's true, had brought sandwiches with them, but they weren't going to share them with a rival. They thought to themselves, "No harm in him looking hungry, then the Princess won't have him."

"But Kay, little Kay!" asked Gerda. When did he come? Was he one of all those suitors?"

"All right—give me time! We're just coming to him. It was on the third day— up came a little chap without horse or carriage, stepping out as bold as you please straight up to the palace. His eyes were bright like yours, he had fine thick hair, but apart from that he was shabbily dressed."

"That was Kay!" cried Gerda. "Oh, then I've found him at last," and she clapped her hands joyfully.

"He had a little rucksack," said the crow.

"Ah, I expect that was his toboggan," said Gerda, "for he took one away with him."

"Quite possibly," said the crow. "I didn't look at it at all closely. But I know from my tame sweetheart that, when he came to the palace and saw the bodyguard in silver at the entrance and the lackeys in gold on the stairs, he wasn't in the least put out; he just gave them a nod and said how dull it must be standing on the stairs—he preferred to go inside. There the rooms were blazing with light. Privy Councillors and Ambassadors were going about in bare feet, carrying gold dishes. It was all very grand. His boots squeaked most terribly, but that didn't worry him in the slightest."

"I'm sure that must be Kay," said Gerda. "I know he had new boots on, because I heard them squeaking in Grannie's room."

"Well, they certainly did squeak!" said the crow. "And he went boldly up to the Princess, who was sitting on a pearl as big as a spinning-wheel. All the ladies-in-waiting with their maids and their maids' maids, and all the gentlemen-in-waiting with their footmen and their footmen's footmen who have pages, stood lined up all round; and the nearer they stood to the door, the haughtier they looked. The footmen's footmen's page, who always wears slippers, stands so proudly in the doorway that one can hardly bear to look at him."

"How dreadful!" said little Gerda. "And do you mean to say that Kay has won the Princess?"

"If I hadn't been a crow, I should have taken her myself, even though I'm engaged. He is said to have spoken as well as I speak, when I talk crow language, so my tame sweetheart informs me. He was bold and attractive. He hadn't in the least come to woo the Princess, but merely in order to listen to her wise conversation. He liked her, and she liked him.

"Why, of course, it was Kay," said Gerda. "He was always so clever; he could do mental arithmetic with fractions. Oh, do please take me into the palace."

"Easier said than done," said the crow. "I must talk to my tame sweetheart about it. I daresay she can advise us, for I may as well tell you that a little girl like you will never be allowed right in."

"Yes, I shall," said Gerda. "As soon as Kay hears I am there, he'll come straight out and fetch me."

"Wait for me by that stile," said the crow with a waggle of his head; and away he flew.

It was after dark before he got back. "Rah, rah!" he cawed. "I'm to give you her love, and here's a small loaf for you that she found in the kitchen; they've plenty of bread there, and you must be hungry. You can't possibly be allowed into the palace in those bare feet of yours; the guards in silver and the lackeys in gold would never let you through. But don't cry; you shall get in all right. My sweetheart knows of a little backstair leading to the bedroom, and she knows where to find the key!"

Then they went into the garden, along the great avenue where the leaves were coming down one after another; and as one after another the lights of the palace were going out, the crow took little Gerda round to a backdoor that stood ajar.

Oh, how Gerda's heart went pit-a-pat with

fear and longing! It was just as though she was going to do something wrong; and yet she only wanted to know if this was little Kay. Why, of course it must be him. In her mind she had a living picture of his thick hair, his intelligent eyes; and she could see plainly how he smiled, just as he used to smile when they sat together at home among the roses. She knew how glad he would be to see her, and to hear what a long way she had come for his sake, and how sad they all were at home when he never returned. Yes, she was torn between fear and joy.

Now they had reached the foot of the stairs, where there was a small lamp burning on a shelf. In the middle of the floor stood the tame crow, turning her head this way and that to look at Gerda, who curtsied just as Grannie had taught her.

"My betrothed has spoken so nicely of you, my dear young lady," said the tame crow. "Your biography, as they call it, is really most touching. If you will take the lamp, I will lead the way. Straight ahead is our best way. so as not to meet anyone."

"I feel as if we were being followed," said Gerda; and something whizzed past her that looked like shadows on the wall, horses with tossing manes and scraggy legs, huntsmen, and ladies and gentlemen on horseback.

"They are dreams, that's all," said the tame crow. "They come and fetch Their Highnesses' thoughts away to hunting. That's a good thing, for now you will be able to take a longer look at them while they're asleep. But promise me that, if ever you are raised to honour and dignity, you will show a thankful heart."

"That might better have been left unsaid," said the wild crow.

By now they had got to the first room, where the walls were hung with rose-coloured satin worked with flowers. Here the dreams were already whizzing past so quickly that Gerda hadn't time to see if Their Highnesses were among them. Each room was more magnificent than the last; it was really quite staggering. At length they found themselves in the bedchamber.

The ceiling in here was like a great palm-tree with leaves of glass, precious glass; and over the middle of the floor from a thick stem hung two beds that looked just like lilies. One of them was white; the Princess was sleeping in that one. The other was red, and it was there that Gerda was to look for little Kay. She turned back one of the red leaves and caught sight of a brown neck. It was Kay! She called out his name quite loudly, holding the lamp close to him; the dreams whirled into the room again on horseback; he woke up, turned his head and —it wasn't little Kay at all.

The Prince was only like him in the neck, but he was certainly young and handsome. Meanwhile the Princess peeped out from the white lily-bed and asked what was happening. Then little Gerda burst into tears and told her whole story, and all that the crows had done for her.

"You poor dear!" said the Prince and Princess; and they praised the two crows and told them that they weren't a bit angry with them, but they mustn't do it again. As it was, they should receive a reward. "Would you prefer to fly about on your own," asked the Princess, "or to be given a permanent place as Court Crows, with all the scraps from the kitchen?"

Both crows curtsied and asked for a permanency; they had an eye to the time when they would be getting on in years, and they said it was best to have something laid by "for a rainy day", as the saying is.

The Prince got up and let Gerda have his bed to sleep in; he couldn't do more than that. She folded her little hands, thinking "how kind people and birds are," then shut her eyes and went peacefully to sleep. All the dreams came flying back again, and this time they looked like angels from heaven; they were pulling a little sledge, and on it sat Kay, nodding to her. But the whole thing was only a dream, and so it vanished as soon as she woke up.

The next day she was dressed from head to foot in silk and velvet. She was invited to stay on at the palace and enjoy herself; but all she asked for was a simple horse and carriage and a pair of little boots, and she

338

would drive out into the wide world and find Kay.

She was given both boots and muff and also the most charming clothes; and, as she was ready to leave, there at the door was a new coach of pure gold with the royal arms gleaming on its sides like a star. Coachman, footmen and outriders (for there were outriders as well) all wore gold crowns. The Prince and the Princess themselves helped her into the carriage and wished her every good fortune. The wild crow, who was now married, went with Gerda for the first dozen miles, sitting beside her as he couldn't bear riding back to the horses. The other crow stood in the gateway flapping her wings; she didn't go with them because she suffered from headaches since getting a permanent place and too much to eat. The inside of the coach was lined with sugar twists, and the seat was stuffed with ginger nuts and jujubes.

"Goodbye! Goodbye!" cried Prince and Princess. Little Gerda wept, and the crow wept; and so they drove for some miles. Then it was the crow's turn to say goodbye;

that was the saddest parting of all. He flew up into a tree and flapped his black wings as long as he could still see the coach, glittering there like the clearest sunshine.

5

The little robber girl

As they drove through the dark forest, the coach blazed and sparkled, so that the robbers lying in wait were quite dazzled; it was more than they could bear. "It's gold, it's gold!" they screamed, dashing forward and seizing the horses. They killed the postilions, the coachman and the footmen, and dragged little Gerda out of the carriage.

"She's plump, she's appetizing, she's been fattened on nuts," said the old robber hag,

341

who had a long stiff beard and eyebrows that hung down over her eyes. "She's just like a little fatted lamb. Yum! Won't she taste nice!" And she pulled out her shining knife —it was terrible, the way it glittered.

"Ow!" shrieked the old hag the next instant. She had been bitten in the ear by her own little daughter who was slung on her back, as wild and mischievous as they make them. "You dirty little brat," said the mother, as she missed her chance of slaughtering Gerda.

"She shall play with me," said little robber girl. "She shall give me her muff and her pretty frock, and she shall sleep with me in my bed." And then she gave her mother another bite, so hard that the hag went hopping round and round in her pain, and all the robbers laughed and said, "Look at her dancing with her cub!"

"I want to ride in the coach," said the little robber girl, and she had to have her own way, for she was so spoilt and wilful. So she and Gerda got in, and they drove through stubble and gorse deeper into the forest.

The little robber girl was no bigger than Gerda, but sturdier, with broader shoulders and darker skin. Her eyes were quite black, with a look that was almost sad. She put her arm round little Gerda and said, "They shan't kill you unless I get angry with you. I suppose you're a princess, aren't you?"

"No," said little Gerda and told her all she had been through and how fond she was of little Kay.

The robber girl looked earnestly at her and gave a little nod as she said, "They shan't kill you, even if I do get angry with you; I shall do it myself!" And then she dried Gerda's eyes and put both her hands into the pretty muff that was so soft and warm.

Now the coach stopped. They had drawn up in the courtyard of a robbers' castle. It was full of cracks from top to bottom, ravens and crows flew out of the gaping crevices, while enormous bulldogs, each looking as if it could swallow a man, kept jumping out; but there was no barking, as that was not allowed.

A big fire was burning in the middle of the stone floor of the huge grimy old hall; the smoke trailed along under the ceiling, trying to find its way out. A great saucepan of soup was on the boil, and both hares and rabbits were turning on the spit.

"You shall sleep here to-night with me and all my pets," said the robber girl. They got something to eat and drink, and they went over to a corner where there were rugs and straw. On laths and perches above their heads nearly a hundred pigeons were roosting, apparently all asleep, but they did just stir when the two small girls came in.

"They're all mine," said the little robber girl, catching hold of one of the nearest. She took it by the legs and shook it till it flapped its wings. "Give her a kiss!" she cried and flipped Gerda in the face with it. Then, pointing to a number of bars placed in front of a hole high up in the wall, "There are the bad lads of the forest," she went on, "behind those bars. Those two, they'd fly away at once, if they weren't properly locked up. And here's my old sweetheart, Moo," she added, lugging out by its horns a reindeer which was tied up by means of a shiny copper ring round its neck. "He's another we have to keep a tight hold on, or he'd soon go loping off. Every blessed evening I tickle his neck for him with my sharp knife—he doesn't care for that!" And the child drew a long knife out of a crack in the wall and ran it lightly along the reindeer's neck. The poor creature let fly with its hoofs and, with a laugh, the robber girl drew Gerda down with her into bed.

"Do you always sleep with your knife beside you?" asked Gerda, looking at it rather nervously.

"Yes, I always sleep with a knife," answered the little robber girl. "You never know what may happen. But now tell me again what you told me before about little Kay and why you started out into the wide, wide world." So Gerda told her all over again, and the wood-pigeons cooed up in their cage, and the other pigeons slept. The little robber girl, with one arm round Gerda's neck and the other holding the knife, went to sleep—you could hear that—but Gerda simply couldn't close her eyes; she hardly knew whether she was to live or die. The robbers sat round the fire, singing and drinking, while the old hag turned somersaults. It was a ghastly sight for the little girl.

Then the wood-pigeons said, "Roo-cool! Roo-cool! we have seen little Kay. A white hen was carrying his toboggan. Kay was sitting in the Snow Queen's sledge, as it skimmed over the wood where we lay in our nest. She breathed down on us young ones, who all died except us two. Roo-cool! Roo-cool!"

"What's that you're saying up there?" Gerda called out. "Where was the Snow Queen going? Do you know anything about that?"

"She must have been making for Lapland, because they've got snow and ice up there. Ask the reindeer, who's tied up with a rope; he'll be sure to know."

"Ice and snow, yes," said the reindeer; "it's a lovely country, where you can go bounding to your heart's delight in the great glittering valleys. There the Snow Queen has her summer quarters, but her regular palace is up towards the North Pole on the island called Spitzbergen."

"Poor little Kay!" sighed Gerda.

"Well, now you must lie still," said the robber girl, "or you'll get my knife in your tummy!"

In the morning Gerda told her all that the wood-pigeons had said, and the little robber girl looked quite serious; but she nodded and said, "Never mind, we can manage" and, turning to the reindeer, "Do you know where Lapland is?"

"Who should know better than I?" the animal answered with sparkling eyes. "That's where I was born and bred and first jumped about in the snowfields."

"Now listen," said the robber girl to Gerda. "You see that all our men-folk are away, but Muz is still here, and here she'll stay. Later on she'll take a pull out of that big bottle and after that have a little nap. Then I'll manage something for you." With

347

that she jumped out of bed, gave her mother a hug round the neck and a tug of her moustache, saying, "Good morning, my own darling nanny-goat!" And her mother gave her such a rap under the nose that it turned black and blue, but it was all done purely for love.

As soon as the mother had drunk from the bottle and started her forty winks, the robber girl went to the reindeer and said, "I'm just itching to tickle your neck a lot more with my sharp knife, for then you're so amusing; but never mind, I'm going to let you loose and bring you outside, so that you can run off to Lapland. But you must put your best foot foremost and carry this little girl for me to the Snow Queen's palace, where her playmate is. I expect you heard what she told me, for she talked rather loud, and you're such a one for eavesdropping."

The reindeer simply jumped for joy. The robber girl lifted little Gerda on to his back and took care to strap her on tight—yes, even to give her a little cushion to sit on. "Now you're all right," she said. "You've got your fur-lined boots, for it'll be cold; but I'm keeping the muff, it's too lovely to part with. Still, we mustn't let you feel the cold. Here are my mother's big mittens that come right up to your elbows—there, in you go! Now your hands make you look just like my grubby old mother!" And Gerda wept for joy.

"I can't bear to see you blubbering," said the little robber girl. "Why, you ought to be looking extra pleased. Here's a couple of loaves and a ham, so you shan't starve." Both these were tied on to the reindeer's back. The little robber girl then opened the door, called all the big dogs in and, slashing the rope with her knife, she said to the reindeer, "Off you go! But take great care of the little girl."

Gerda held out her hands, mittens and all, to the little robber girl and said goodbye. And the reindeer flew away across stubble and scrub, through the length of the forest, over bogs and prairies, as fast as he could go. The wolves howled, the ravens squawked. "P—ff! P—ff!" kept coming from the sky; it was just as though it was sneezing red.

"They're my dear old Northern Lights,"
said the reindeer. "Look how they sparkle!"
And then he ran on faster than ever, night
and day. The loaves were eaten up, and the
ham too; and at last they were in Lapland.

6

The Lapp woman and the Finn woman

They halted at a small house, such a miserable place. The roof came right down to the ground, and the doorway was so low that the family had to crawl in and out on their stomachs. Nobody was at home except an old Lapp woman who stood frying fish over an oil-lamp. The reindeer told her all about Gerda—but, first, all about himself, as he felt that was much more important, and Gerda was too done up with the cold to be able to speak.

"Oh, you poor things!" said the Lapp

woman. "You've a long way to go yet. You must cover hundreds of miles before you get to the Finmark—that's where the Snow Queen has a country seat and burns Roman candles every single evening. I'll write a few words on a piece of dried cod, for I haven't got any paper, and you can take it along with you to the Finn woman up there; she can tell you better than I can what to do."

By this time Gerda had warmed up and had something to eat and drink, so the Lapp woman wrote a few words on a piece of dried cod and told Gerda to mind and take care of it. Then she strapped her tight again on to the reindeer and off they went. "P—ff! P—ff!" they heard spluttering in the sky, and all night long they saw the loveliest blue Northern Lights burning. At last they reached the Finmark and knocked on the Finn woman's chimney, for she hadn't even a door. Inside, the air was so hot that the Finn woman herself went about with hardly a stitch of clothing. She was dumpy and dark-skinned. She at once loosened little Gerda's clothes and took off her mittens and boots, otherwise she would have been much too warm; she also put a lump of ice on the reindeer's head, and after that she read what was written on the dried cod. She read it over three times, till she knew it by heart, and then she popped the fish into the stock-pot, for it was quite eatable and she never wasted anything.

First, the reindeer told his own story, and then little Gerda's; and the Finn woman's knowing eyes twinkled, but she didn't say a word.

"You're so clever," said the reindeer. "I know you can tie up all the winds in the world with a thread of cotton. If the skipper undoes one knot, he gets a good wind; if he undoes a second, it blows hard; and when he undoes the third and the fourth, there's a gale that sends the trees of the forest crash-ing. Will you give this little girl a drink that will lend her the strength of twelve men, so that she can get the better of the Snow Queen?"

"The strength of twelve men?" said the

Finn woman; "I'm afraid that wouldn't go far!" Then she went over to a shelf and took down a big rolled-up parchment, which she unrolled. There was strange writing on it, and the Finn woman stood reading it till the sweat poured from her forehead.

But the reindeer pleaded again so hard for little Gerda, and Gerda looked with such tearful beseeching eyes at the Finn woman, that the twinkle came back into hers and, drawing the reindeer into a corner, she put a fresh lump of ice on his head and had a whispered conversation with him.

"Yes, it's quite true, little Kay is with the Snow Queen and finds everything to his liking and thinks it's the nicest place in the world; but that's only because he's got a glass splinter in his heart and a tiny fragment in his eye. These must come out first, or else he'll never be human again, and the Snow Queen will keep her power over him."

"Well, but isn't there some physic little Gerda can take that will give her power over everything?"

"I can't give her greater power than she

has already. Don't you see how great that is? Don't you see how man and beast feel obliged to serve her, and how far she has come in the world in her bare feet? She mustn't learn of her power from us; it lies in her heart, in her being a dear innocent child. If she can't by herself reach the Snow Queen and get rid of the glass from little Kay, then there's nothing we can do to help. The Snow Queen's garden begins about ten miles further on. You can carry the little girl so far, then set her down close to the large bush with red berries that's standing there in the snow. Don't stay gossiping, but make haste back here." Then the Finn woman lifted little Gerda on to the back of the reindeer, who dashed off as fast as he could.

"Oh, I've forgotten my boots! I've forgotten my mittens!" little Gerda called out, directly she felt the piercing cold. But the reindeer didn't dare stop; he ran on till he came to the large bush with the red berries. There he put Gerda down and kissed her on the mouth; big shining tears ran down the animal's cheeks, and then back he dashed once more as fast as he could go. There was poor Gerda, left standing without shoes, without gloves, in the middle of the terrible icy Finmark.

She started running forward as well as she could, but then a whole regiment of snowflakes appeared. They didn't fall from the sky, for that was quite clear and glittering with Northern Lights. The snowflakes came running along the ground, and the nearer they came, the bigger they grew. Gerda remembered no doubt how big and curious they had looked that time she saw them through the burning-glass; but these were altogether bigger and more terrifying—they were alive, they were the Snow Queen's advance-guards, they had the most fantastic shapes. Some of them looked like vicious great hedgehogs, others like a lot of knotted snakes sticking out their heads, and others like fat little bears with bristling pelts; all of them were glittering white, all of them living snowflakes.

Then little Gerda said the Lord's Prayer, and the cold was so intense that she could

356

see her own breath coming just like smoke out of her mouth; it grew thicker and thicker, until it took the shape of little shining angels who got bigger and bigger as they touched the ground. They all had helmets on their heads, and spears and shields in their hands. Their numbers grew and grew and, by the time Gerda had finished her prayer, there was a whole legion of them around her. They struck with their spears at the horrible snow-flakes, so that they flew into a hundred pieces, and little Gerda could walk on without fear or danger. The angels patted her feet and hands for her, so that she didn't feel the cold so much and was able to walk briskly on towards the Snow Queen's palace ...

But now it's time for us to see how Kay is getting on. It's quite certain he hasn't given a thought to Gerda; least of all does he imagine that she's standing outside the palace.

7

What happened at the Snow Queen's palace and afterwards

The walls of the palace were built of drifting snow, and the windows and doors of cutting winds. There were over a hundred rooms, just as the blizzards had made them, the largest stretching out for miles, all of them lit up by the vivid Northern Lights: huge, empty, ice-cold and glittering. Never was there any jollification, not even so much as a little dance for the bears, when the gale could play the horn and the polar-bears

358

get up on their hind-legs and show off their party manners. Never a little social with mouth-slapping and paw-rapping; never the smallest tea-fight for the snowy young vixens; all was bare, bleak and vast in the halls of the Snow Queen. The Northern Lights flared up each time so punctually that you could work out just when they would be at their highest point and when at their lowest. In the middle of the empty unending snow-hall lay a frozen lake. It was cracked into a thousand pieces, but each piece looked so exactly like the other that it was quite a work of art. It was here, in the middle, that the Snow Queen would sit, when she was at home; she would say that she was sitting at the Glass of Reason, and that was the one and only glass in the world.

Little Kay was quite blue with cold, in fact, almost black. But he never noticed it, because the Snow Queen had kissed the cold shivers out of him, and his heart was little more than a lump of ice. He was engaged in dragging along some sharp-edged flat pieces of ice, which he was trying in all sorts of positions; he wanted to make some kind of pattern from them, in the same way as we arrange little wooden pieces when we do a jig-saw puzzle. Kay, too, was busy with patterns, most complicated ones; it was the Great Mental Ice Puzzle. To him these patterns seemed most remarkable and highly important; that was the result of the glass splinter in his eye. He put together whole patterns which made up a written word, but he never could manage the one word he was after—the word ETERNITY. And yet the Snow Queen had said to him, "If you can find me that pattern, then you shall be your own master, and I'll make you a present of the whole world and a pair of new skates." But he just couldn't.

"Now I must tear off to the warm countries," said the Snow Queen. "I want to go and peep into the black pots." She meant the burning mountains that we call Etna and Vesuvius. "I shall whiten them a little—one generally has to; it does them good after all the lemons and grapes." So the Snow Queen flew off, and Kay was left looking at the

360

pieces of ice and thinking, thinking, until he was quite dizzy. There he sat, quite still, without moving a muscle; you might have thought he was frozen to death.

It was at this moment that Gerda walked into the palace through the great gate of cutting winds. But she said an evening prayer, and the winds died down as if they were sleepy, and she stepped into the great empty shivery halls—there was Kay! She knew him at once, rushed and flung her arms round his neck and held him tight, exclaiming, "Kay, dear, darling Kay! I've found you at last!"

But he sat there quite still, all cold and stiff ... Then little Gerda wept hot tears— they fell on his breast, they forced their way into his heart, they thawed out the lump of ice and dissolved the little bit of glass that was there. He looked at her, and she sang the words of the hymn:

"The valley glows with many a rose,
  and there we meet the Sacred Child."

Then Kay burst into tears. He cried so much

that the splinter of glass trickled out of his eye; he recognised her and shouted joyfully, "Gerda, dear, darling Gerda! Where ever have you been all this time? And where have I been?" Then he looked about him. "How cold it is! How empty and huge!" And he kept tight hold of Gerda, while she laughed and cried for joy. They were so happy that even the flat pieces of ice danced with delight and, when they got tired and calmed down, there they were forming the very word that the Snow Queen had said Kay must find out, then he should be his own master and she would give him the whole world and a pair of new skates.

And Gerda kissed his cheeks, and they bloomed once more. She kissed his eyes, and they sparkled like hers. She kissed his hands and feet, and he was well and strong again. Let the Snow Queen come home now if she liked—there was his release, written out in glittering ice.

Then hand in hand they wandered out of the vast palace, talking about Grannie and the roses up on the roof. Wherever they went, the winds died down and the sun broke through; and when they got to the bush with the red berries, there was the reindeer waiting for them. He had a young doe with him; her udders were full of warm milk for the two children, and she kissed them on the mouth. They took Kay and Gerda on their backs and carried them, first, to the Finn woman, where they warmed themselves in her hot room and were told about the way home, and after that to the Lapp woman, who had made some new clothes for them and put her sledge in repair.

The reindeer and the young doe bounded alongside and kept with them as far as the frontier, where the first green shoots were beginning to peep out. There Kay and Gerda parted from the reindeer and the Lapp woman, and they all said goodbye to each other. And now the first little birds were beginning to twitter, the first green buds to appear in the forest; and out of it came a young girl riding a magnificent horse, which Gerda remembered seeing harnessed to the gold coach. The young girl had a bright red cap on her head and pistols at her belt. It was the little robber girl, who was tired of being at home and was now making for the North; but if she didn't like it there, she was going to try somewhere else. She recognised Gerda immediately, and Gerda recognised her; they were overjoyed.

"You're a queer sort of globe-trotter!" she said to little Kay. "I wonder if you're worth running after to the ends of the earth."

But Gerda patted her cheek and asked after the Prince and Princess.

"They've gone abroad," said the robber girl.

"Well, but what about the crow?" asked Gerda. "Ah, the crow's dead," she answered. "The tame sweetheart's a widow now and goes about with a bit of black wool round her leg. She's terribly sorry for herself, but it's all put on. Well, now tell me all about yourself, and how you managed to get hold of Kay."

Then Gerda and Kay between them told her the whole story. "And snip, snap, snout, your tale is out!" said the robber girl. She shook hands with them both and promised that, if ever she passed through their town, she would come up and pay them a call; and then away she rode into the wide world.

But Kay and Gerda walked on hand in hand and, as they went, spring came to meet them in all its beauty of blossom and greenery. The church bells rang out, and they recognized the tall steeples and the large town —it was the very one they lived in. And they went into the town, straight along to their grandmother's door, up the stairs, and into the room, where everything was just as they left it and the clock said, "tick, tick" and the hands were still going round. But as they went through the door they noticed they were now grown up. The roses in the boxes over the gutter were beginning to flower at the open windows, and their own little stools were still in their place. So Kay and Gerda sat down and took each other by the hand. The cold empty splendour of the Snow Queen's palace was now forgotten like a bad dream. Grannie was sitting there in God's clear sunshine, reading aloud from the

Bible, "Except ye become as little children, ye shall not enter into the Kingdom of Heaven."

Kay and Gerda looked into each other's eyes, and all at once they understood the meaning of the old hymn:

"The valley glows with many a rose,
and there we meet the Sacred Child."

There they sat, the two of them, grown up and yet children—children at heart. And it was summertime, warm delicious summertime.

THE RED SHOES

There was once a little girl, very delicate and pretty, and yet so poor that in summer she always had to go barefooted and in winter she had to wear big wooden clogs which chafed her insteps most horribly, until they were quite red.

In the middle of the village lived a shoemaker's widow, who had some strips of old red cloth, and out of these she did her best to sew a little pair of shoes. They were rather clumsy-looking shoes, but the old widow meant well; they were for the little girl, whose name was Karen. As it happened, she got the red shoes and put them on for the first time on the very day that her mother was buried. Of course they weren't exactly the right shoes for a funeral, but they were the only ones she had; and so she wore them on her bare feet, as she followed the humble straw coffin.

Just then a large old-looking carriage drove up with a large old-looking lady inside it. She caught sight of the little girl and felt sorry for her. So she said to the parson: "Look here, if you let me have the little girl, I'll take care of her."

Karen thought this was all because of the red shoes, but the old lady said they were hideous and had them burnt; Karen herself was given nice new clothes and was taught to read and sew. People said how pretty she was, but the looking-glass said to her: "You are more than pretty, you are lovely."

On one occasion the Queen was passing through the country with her little daughter, who was a Princess. People flocked around the castle, and Karen was there too; and the little Princess shewed herself at one of the windows. She was wearing a beautiful white dress; no train nor golden crown, but lovely red morocco shoes—far, far prettier than the ones the shoemaker's widow had made for little Karen. No, there was really nothing in the world like red shoes.

By now Karen was old enough to be confirmed. She was given new clothes, and she was also to have new shoes. The best shoemaker in town took the measurement of her feet in his own private room, where there were big glass cabinets with elegant shoes and shiny boots. They made a brave show, but the old lady's sight was far from good, and so it gave her no pleasure. Among the shoes was a red pair just like the ones the Princess had been wearing—oh, they were pretty! The shoemaker explained that they had been made for an earl's daughter but didn't quite fit. "That must be patent leather from the way they shine," said the old lady.

"Yes, don't they shine!" said Karen; and as they were a good fit, the shoes were bought. But the old lady didn't realise that they were red, for she would never have allowed Karen to go to Confirmation in red shoes. And yet that's just what happened.

Everybody stared at her feet and, as she walked up the aisle to the chancel, she felt that even the old pictures over the tombs, those portraits of the clergy and their wives in stiff ruffs and long black garments, were fastening their eyes on the red shoes. It was these that filled her thoughts, when the priest laid his hand on her head and spoke of holy baptism, of the covenant with God, and of her duty now to become a fully-fledged Christian. And the organ played so solemnly, and the children sang so beautifully, and the old choirmaster sang, too; but Karen thought of nothing but her red shoes.

By the afternoon, sure enough, the old lady had heard from everybody about the shoes being red, and she said how shocking it was; they were quite out of place and in future, when Karen went to church, she must always wear black shoes, however old they were.

370

Next Sunday there was Communion, and Karen looked at the black shoes, and she looked at the red ones ... And then she looked at the red ones again—and put the red ones on.

It was a beautiful sunny day. Karen and the old lady took the path through the cornfield, where it was a bit dusty. At the church-door stood an old soldier with a crutch and a funny long beard which was more red than white—in fact, it really was red. He made a deep bow to the old lady and asked if he might dust her shoes. And when Karen also put out her foot, "My! what lovely dancing-shoes!" said the soldier. "Stay on tight when you dance!" and he gave the soles a tap with his hand.

The old lady gave the soldier something for himself and went with Karen into the church. The whole congregation stared at Karen's red shoes, and so did all the por-traits; and when Karen knelt before the altar and put the gold chalice to her lips, she thought of nothing but the red shoes—it seemed as if they were floating in front of her. She forgot to sing the hymns, and she forgot to say the prayers.

Presently everyone came out of church, and the old lady stepped into her carriage. As Karen raised her foot to get in after her, the old soldier, who was standing close by, said: "My! what lovely dancing-shoes!" Karen couldn't resist—she had to dance a few steps and, once she had started, her feet went on dancing just as though the shoes had some power over them. She danced round the corner of the church—she couldn't stop; the coachman had to run after her and pick her up and carry her back into the carriage. But still her feet went on dancing and gave the kind old lady some dreadful kicks. At last they got the shoes off, and her legs kept still.

When they came home, the shoes were put away in a cupboard, but Karen still kept taking a peep at them. By and by the old lady fell ill; it was said she would never get better. She had to be nursed and cared for, and nobody was more suited for this than Karen. But a big ball was being given in the town, and Karen was invited. She looked at the old lady, who after all couldn't live long, and she looked at the red shoes. She couldn't see there would be any harm. She put on the red shoes, she had a perfect right to do that ... But then she went to the ball and began to dance.

But when she wanted to go to the right, the shoes went dancing off to the left; and when she wanted to go up the room, the shoes went dancing down the room—down the stairs through the street and out by the town-gate. Dance she did and dance she must, away into the dark forest.

Up among the trees she saw something shining. It looked like a face, and so she thought it was the moon; but it was the old soldier with the red beard, sitting and nodding and saying: "My! what lovely dancing-shoes!"

This made her frightened, and she tried to kick off the red shoes, but they still stuck on tight. She tore off her stockings, but the shoes had grown fast to her feet, and so dance she did and dance she must, over field and furrow, in rain and sun, by night and day; but the night-time was the worst.

She danced into the open churchyard, but the dead there didn't dance; they had something better to do. She wanted to sit down by the poor man's grave, where the bitter tansy grew; but peace and quiet were not for her and, when she danced towards the open church-door, she found an angel there in long white robes and with wings reaching from his shoulders to the ground. His face was stern and solemn, and in his hand he held a sword with broad shining blade.

"Dance you shall," said the angel, "dance in your red shoes until you are cold and pale, until your skin shrivels up like a skeleton's! Dance you shall from door to door, and at all the houses where the children are vain and proud you shall knock till they hear you and are frightened. You shall dance, you shall dance ...!"

"Mercy! Mercy!" cried Karen. But she never heard the angel's answer, for the shoes whirled her away through the gate and the field, along highway and byway, dancing, dancing, all the time.

One morning she danced past a door she knew well. From inside came the sound of a hymn; then out came a coffin all covered with flowers. She realised then that the old lady was dead, and she felt that now she was deserted by everyone, as well as cursed by the angel of God.

Dance she did and dance she must, dance on in the dark night ... The shoes whirled her away over thorns and stubble, until she was scratched and bleeding. She danced across the heath up to a lonely little house. She knew that the executioner lived here, and she rapped the window-pane with her knuckles and said: "Please come out! I can't come in, because I'm dancing."

"Do you mean to say you don't know who I am? I cut off wicked people's heads —my goodness, how my axe is quivering!"

"Please don't cut off my head!" said Karen, "for then I can't show that I'm sorry for my sins. Cut off my feet with the red shoes."

Then she confessed all her sins, and the executioner cut off her feet with the red shoes. But the shoes went dancing with the little feet across the fields into the depths of the forest. And he made her wooden feet and crutches; he taught her a hymn—the Psalm for Sinners—and she kissed the hand that had wielded the axe and went her way across the heath.

"Surely by now I must have done penance for the red shoes," she said. "I'll go to church and let everyone see me." And she did; she went quickly towards the church-door but, when she reached it, there were the red shoes dancing in front of her, and she grew frightened and turned back.

All the next week she was miserable and did nothing but cry, but when Sunday came round she said to herself: "Dear me, I really feel I've been through enough. Surely I'm just as good as many of those that sit so perkily there in church." And she plucked up her courage and started off, but she got no further than the gate, when she saw the red shoes dancing in front of her, and she grew frightened and turned back and repented deeply of her sins.

Next she made her way to the parsonage and asked to be taken in there as a servant; she would work so hard and do her very best. She never gave a thought to the wages, only that she might have a roof over her head and be with kind people.

The parson's wife felt sorry for her and took her into her service and found her hard-working and sensible. In the evenings Karen sat and listened in silence, while the parson read aloud from the Bible. All the little ones were very fond of her but, when there was talk of dress and finery and of being as pretty as a picture, she would shake her head.

The following Sunday they all went to church, and they asked her to go with them; but with tears in her eyes she looked sadly at her crutches and, when the others went off to hear the word of God, she went alone to her tiny room, where there was just enough space for a bed and a chair, and here she sat devoutly reading her prayer-book. As she did so, the wind brought the sound of the organ to her from the church, and her eyes filled with tears as she lifted up her face, exclaiming: "Help me, O God!"

Then the sun came out so brightly, and straight in front of her stood the same angel in white robes that she had seen that night at the church-door. But instead of the sharp sword he was holding a beautiful green bough that was covered with roses; and he touched the ceiling with it so that it arched itself higher, and where he touched it there shone a golden star. And he touched the walls so that they grew wider; and she saw the organ which was still playing, she saw the old pictures of the clergy and their wives, and the congregation sitting in the carved pews and singing from their hymn-books ... You see, the church itself had come to the poor girl in her narrow little room—or was it she who had come to the church? She was sitting in the pew with all the others from the parsonage and, when they had finished the hymn and looked up from their books, they nodded to her and said: "It was right you should come, Karen." "It was God's mercy!" she answered.

And the organ pealed forth and the young voices of the choir sounded so soft and pure. The bright warm sunshine streamed in through the church-window to the place where Karen was sitting. Her heart was so full of sunshine and peace and joy that at last it broke, and her soul flew on the sunbeams to heaven, where there was no one to ask about the red shoes.

THE LITTLE MATCH-SELLER

It was terribly cold. Snow was falling. and soon it would be quite dark; for it was the last day in the year—New Year's Eve. Along the street, in that same cold and dark, went a poor little girl in bare feet— well, yes, it's true, she had slippers on when she left home; but what was the good of that? They were great big slippers which her mother used to wear, so you can imagine the size of them; and they both came off when the little girl scurried across the road

380

just as two carts went whizzing by at a fearful rate. One slipper was not to be found, and a boy ran off with the other, saying it would do for a cradle one day when he had children of his own.

So there was the little girl, walking along in her bare feet that were simply blue with cold. In an old apron she was carrying a whole lot of matches, and she had one bunch of them in her hand. She hadn't sold anything all day, and no one had given her a single penny. Poor mite, she looked so downcast, as she trudged along hungry and shivering. The snowflakes settled on her long flaxen hair, which hung in pretty curls over her shoulders; but you may be sure she wasn't thinking about her looks. Lights were shining in every window, and out into the street came the lovely smell of roast goose. You see, it was New Year's Eve; that's what she was thinking about.

Over in a little corner between two houses —one of them jutted out rather more into the street than the other—there she crouched and huddled with her legs tucked under her; but she only got colder and colder. She didn't dare to go home, for she hadn't sold a match nor earned a single penny. Her father would beat her, and besides it was so cold at home. They had only the bare roof over their heads and the wind whistled through that, although the worst cracks had been stopped up with rags and straw. Her hands were really quite numb with cold. Ah, but a little match—that would be a comfort. If only she dared pull one out of the bunch, just one, strike it on the wall and warm her fingers! She pulled one out . . . ritch! . . . how it spirted and blazed! Such a clear warm flame, like a little candle, as she put her hand round it—yes, and what a curious light it was! The little girl fancied she was sitting in front of a big iron stove with shiny brass knobs and brass facings, with such a warm friendly fire burning . . . why, whatever was that? She was just stretching out her toes, so as to warm them too, when—out went the flame, and the stove vanished. There she sat with a little stub of burnt-out match in her hand.

She struck another one. It burned up so brightly, and where the gleam fell on the wall this became transparent like gauze. She could see right into the room, where the table was laid with a glittering white cloth and with delicate china; and there, steaming deliciously, was the roast goose stuffed with prunes and apples. Then, what was even finer, the goose jumped off the dish and waddled along the floor with the carving-knife and fork in its back. Right up to the poor little girl it came ... but then the match went out, and nothing could be seen but the massive cold wall.

She lighted another match. Now she was sitting under the loveliest Christmas tree; it was even bigger and prettier than the one she had seen through the glass-door at the rich merchant's at Christmas. Hundreds of candles were burning on the green branches, and gay-coloured prints, like the ones they hang in the shop-windows, looked down at her. The little girl reached up both her hands ... then the match went out; all the Christmas candles rose higher and higher, until now she could see they were the shining stars. One of them rushed down the sky with a long fiery streak.

"That's somebody dying," said the little girl; for her dead Grannie, who was the only one who had been kind to her, had told her that a falling star shows that a soul is going up to God.

She struck yet another match on the wall. It gave a glow all around, and there in the midst of it stood her old grandmother, looking so very bright and gentle and loving. "Oh, Grannie", cried the little girl, "do take me with you! I know you'll disappear as soon as the match goes out — just as the warm stove did, and the lovely roast goose, and the wonderful great Christmas-tree". And she quickly struck the rest of the matches in the bunch, for she did so want to keep her Grannie there. And the matches flared up so gloriously that it became brighter than broad daylight. Never had Grannie looked so tall and beautiful. She took the little girl into her arms, and together they flew in joy and splendour, up, up, to where there was no cold, no hunger, no fear. They were with God.

But in the cold early morning huddled between the two houses, sat the little girl with rosy cheeks and a smile on her lips, frozen to death on the last night of the old year. The New Year dawned on the little dead body leaning there with the matches, one lot of them nearly all used up. "She was trying to get warm", people said. Nobody knew what lovely things she had seen and in what glory she had gone with her old Grannie to the happiness of the New Year.

1₂₅

SIMPLE SIMON

(a nursery tale retold)

Away in the country, in an old manor-house, lived an old squire. He had two sons who were so clever that—well, the fact is they were too clever by half. They made up their minds to go and propose to the King's daughter; and they had a perfect right to do this, because she had announced that she would marry the man who she thought was best able to speak up for himself.

The two sons now spent a week in preparation. A week was all they were allowed; but it was quite long enough, for they had had a good education. and that is such a help. One of them knew the whole Latin dictionary off by heart, and also the local newspaper for the last three years, both backwards and forwards. The other son had learnt up all the by-laws of the city companies and the things every alderman is supposed to know; he thought this would help him to talk politics with the Princess; and, besides, he knew how to embroider braces, he was so very clever with his fingers.

"I shall win the Princess!" cried both of them; and so their father gave them each a beautiful horse. The brother who had learnt off the dictionary and the newspapers got a coal-black horse; and the one who knew all about aldermen and could do embroidery got a milk-white horse; and then they smeared the corners of their mouths with cod-liver oil, so that the words would come out pat. All the servants were down in the courtyard to see them mount their horses, when just at that moment up came the third brother; for there were three of them, though nobody ever took count of the third, because he wasn't a scholar like the other two. They called him Simple Simon.

"Where are you two off to in that get-up?" he asked.

"We're going to Court, to talk our way into favour with the Princess. Haven't you heard the proclamation that's been read out all over the country?" And then they told him all about it.

"Gosh! I mustn't miss this!" said Simple Simon. But his brothers laughed at him and rode away.

"Dad, let me have a horse!" cried Simple Simon. "I do so feel like getting married. If she'll have me, she'll have me; and if she won't, then I'll marry her all the same."

"What nonsense!" said the father. "I've no horse for you. Why, you never open your mouth. But look at your brothers—they are splendid fellows."

"If I can't have a horse," said the boy, "then I'll ride the billy-goat. It's my own, and it'll carry me all right, I know." Then he got astride the billy-goat, dug his heels into its sides and dashed off down the road. Phew! What a rate they went! "Look out! Here we come!" yelled Simple Simon, and his cries went echoing after him.

But his brothers rode on ahead in complete silence. They never said a word, because they had to turn over in their minds all the clever remarks they were going to make. It had to be most cunningly worked out, I can tell you.

"Tally-ho!" shouted Simple Simon, "here we are! Look what I found on the road," and he shewed them a dead crow he had picked up.

"You simpleton!" they said. "What are you going to do with that?"

"I shall give it to the Princess."

"Yes, do!" they answered, laughing as they rode on.

"Tally-ho! Here we are! Now look what I've found. You don't find that on the road every day."

The brothers turned round again to see

what it was. "You simpleton!" they said. "Why, that's an old clog with the vamp missing. Is the Princess to have that as well?"

"Yes, of course," said Simple Simon; and his brothers only laughed at him and rode on till they were a long way ahead.

"Tally-ho! Here we are!" shouted Simon. "My word! This is getting better and better. Tally-ho! This is grand!"

"What have you found this time?" asked the brothers.

"Oh, it's too good for anything," said Simple Simon. "Won't she be pleased, the Princess!"

"Ugh!" said the brothers. "Why, it's mud straight out of the ditch."

"Yes, that's just what it is," said Simple Simon, "and the very finest sort, too; it slips right through your fingers." And he filled his pocket with the mud.

But his two brothers rode on as hard as they could go, and the result was that they drew up at the city gate a whole hour ahead of him and found the suitors being given numbers in the order of their arrival. They were made to stand in rows, six in each file, and so close together that they couldn't move their arms. This was just as well, for otherwise they might have stabbed each other in the back, just because one was in front of the other.

The rest of the inhabitants all crowded round the castle, right up against the windows, so as to watch the Princess receiving her suitors; but as soon as ever one of them came into her presence, he was completely tongue-tied. "No good!" the Princess kept saying. "Skedaddle!"

Now it was the turn of the brother who knew the dictionary by heart. But he had clean forgotten it while he was standing in the queue; and the floor creaked under him, and the ceiling was all covered with mirrors, so that he saw himself standing on his head. At the window stood three clerks and an alderman, who all wrote down every word that was spoken, so that it could go straight into the newspaper and be sold for a penny at the street-corner. It was dreadful; and,

what's more, they had made up such a fire
that the stove was red-hot.

"It's very warm in here," said the suitor.

"That's because my father's roasting cockerels to-day." said the Princess.

"O-o-oh!" was all he could say, as he stood
there. He hadn't expected a remark like that,
and he was hoping to say something witty.
"O-o-oh!"

"No good!" said the Princess. "Skedaddle!"
—and away he had to go. After that the second brother came in.

"It's dreadfully hot in here," he said.

"Yes, we're roasting cockerels for dinner,"
said the Princess.

"I b-beg your—b-beg your—" he stutt-
ered; and the clerks all wrote down "I b-beg
your—b-beg your—"

"No good!" said the Princess. "Skedaddle!"

Now it was Simple Simon's turn. He came
trotting in on the billygoat, right into the
palace-room. "Why, it's as hot as blazes in
here!" he said.

"That's because I'm roasting cockerels,"
said the Princess.

"Oh, I say, that's lucky," said Simple Simon. "So I suppose I can have a crow roasted, can't I!"

"Of course you can, quite easily," said the Princess; "but have you got anything to roast it in, for I've neither pot nor pan."

"But I have," said Simon. "Here's a cooker with a tin handle!' And he produced the old clog and popped the crow straight into it.

"It will make quite a meal," said the Princess. "But what shall we do for gravy?"

"I've got that in my pocket," said Simon. "I've enough and to spare." And he tipped a little mud out of his pocket.

"I do like that!" said the Princess. "You know how to answer; you can speak up for yourself, and you're the one I'm going to marry! But do you realise that every word we've been saying has been written down and will be in the papers to-morrow? Look there by the window—three clerks and an old alderman; and the alderman is the worst, because he doesn't understand a thing." Of course she said this just to frighten him. And the clerks all guffawed and made a great blot of ink on the floor.

"So these are the gentry?" said Simon. "Well, here's one for the alderman!" And he turned out his pocket and let him have the mud full in the face.

"Well done!" cried the Princess. "I could never have done that, but I'll soon learn." So in the end Simple Simon became King, with a wife of his own and a crown and a throne. And all this comes sthaight out of the alderman's newspaper; so it may not be perfectly true!